*'his Kette
to have love
+ lost...*

OUR bLacK HEARts bEat as ONE

bRIAN ASMAN

A MUTATED MEDIA PRODUCTION

Our Black Hearts Beat As One
Copyright © 2023 Brian Asman

Edited by Candace Nola and Mort Stone

Cover Art by Kristina Osborn

Interior Layout by Lori Michelle
www.TheAuthorsAlley.com

Queen of Pain
Words and Music by Matthew Thomas Skiba, Daniel Andriano and Derek Grant
Copyright © 2023 BMG Gold Songs and Hell Toupee
All Rights Administered by BMG Rights Management (US) LLC.
All Rights Reserved Used by Permission
Reprinted by Permission of Hal Leonard LLC

Also by Brian Asman

I'm Not Even Supposed to be Here Today
(Eraserhead Press)
Jailbroke
Nunchuck City
Man, Fuck This House
Return Of the Living Elves

Coming Soon

Good Dogs (Blackstone)

For the heartbroken

"Gamoa and Nanioul, Karphas, Fek and Puez,
Bellies full-bursting from the only meal they've been fed,
From tomb-depths and prison-abyss,
All have a place in preparing thy mother's table."
—Ancient Terrine Proverb

"If we kill the divine, do we kill ourselves?"
—Modern Love, "Liminal Gods"

"The stars at night are big and bright
Deep in your eyes, Miss Vincent
You told me once I made you smile
We both know damn well I didn't."
—Alkaline Trio, "Queen of Pain"

Diamet

DIAMET

"IT'S NOT WORKING."

Kara, cross-armed in the kitchen, half-glass of wine on the counter.

Mike, barely over the threshold, front door open at his back.

He paused, holding a bouquet of redagalias from the Truxton Market, his weathered army jacket damp from the afternoon drizzle. Eyed the microwave, the toaster, the stove. Things were always breaking—cost of living in a pre-war apartment in the Arts District. Spacious but dated. Beautiful but unreliable. Most nights they'd go out on the fire escape with a bottle of wine and smoke challa, listening to buskers play—sometimes one of Mike's songs—watching couples just like them pass by, arm-in-arm, baskers in a bespoke world.

"Is it the TV again?" Mike asked. "You just need to do the thing—"

Kara shook her head, long dark hair splashing about. Lifted her wine glass.

Ended it.

"We're not working." Kara set the empty glass on the counter. She stood there, fiddling with the tantagram she always wore about her throat.

Mike stared at her. "We're not?"

The flowers fell from his hands.

Kara's shoulders hitched, once, like a stifled sob. Then

I

she brushed past him, stepping around the redagalias on the carpet.

Slung her bag over her shoulder—the big leather one.

"I'm sorry," she said, looking down the hall. "The movers will be here within the hour."

And left.

By the time he thought to run after her, the hallway was empty. The stairwell too.

Out on the street, a busker huddled beneath an empty storefront, playing "Egomancy" on a tuneless guitar while a light drizzle speckled the sidewalk.

Mike whipped his head back and forth, desperately.

But she was already gone.

Back in the apartment. He tried her phone—disconnected. Ignored the flowers on the floor and moved quickly through their two bedrooms, checking the closets, the bathtub, as if this were a joke, a game. Hide and go seek.

The cardboard boxes, contents scrawled in marker on their sides, avowed it wasn't a joke. Seconded by the disassembled bedframe, the mattress plastic-wrapped and leaned against the wall.

How long was he gone? Two hours, three?

He kept thinking about the minutes before he went out—Kara in the second bedroom, her studio. Painting. Why they got along so well for the past three years. He was a musician, she, an artist. Oils, mostly. Geometric shapes, complex lined patterns that looked straight from afar, but bowed and bent at close range.

She set her paintbrush down when he came in.

"I'm meeting Keegs and Donnie for a drink," Mike had said. "You want to come?"

Kara gestured at her painting. "On a roll here. Besides, it'll just be band talk, anyway."

He couldn't fault her that—when he got together with

Keegan and Donnie, Modern Love was nearly all they talked about. Future gigs, when they were practicing, the new album they hoped to record. Didn't help he got recognized so often, either, but Modern Love was the biggest thing to come out of the City in years. Everybody felt like they had a stake.

"K," he said, and kissed her, and it was just like every other kiss they'd ever shared.

Now, standing in an apartment he barely recognized, half the pictures pulled off the walls—she'd patched the nail-holes, white spackle winking at him from across the room—he wondered if that really was their last kiss, and how fucked up it was if he didn't know it as such.

Mike sank to the couch, one of the few pieces of furniture he'd brought when they moved in together.

"What the fuck, Kara. What the fuck."

Someone knocked on the door. Mike twisted around to see he'd left it open. Two thick men in work shirts stood there.

One held a clipboard. "Got an order for 1221 Division, Apt. 9?"

Part of Mike wanted to scream. Push them out, lock the door. If her stuff was still here, this wasn't really happening.

If they took those boxes, the plastic-wrapped bed? She really was gone.

"Yeah," Mike said, and gestured vaguely at the rest of the apartment.

He tried to ignore the men's grunts while they muscled Kara's things out the door, staring at a bright white point of spackle on the wall where one of her favorite pictures used to hang. A Condaire reproduction: a couple picnicking on a riverbank. Behind them, a stand of moss-entangled trees. If you stared long enough, the moss shifted into the impression of a tall man in a Tandsfield hat, watching the couple.

Mike always tried not to stare too long.

"Excuse me."

Mike looked up. One mover was holding the bouquet he'd bought Kara a lifetime ago.

"You want these?"

Dumbly, Mike took the flowers and laid them across his lap.

On the wall, he could almost see the outline of the Condaire print.

Maybe, if he kept watching, he'd pick out the man in the Tandsfield hat, stained to the wall.

He slept on the sofa because he didn't have a bed anymore, wrapped up in towels because all the blankets were hers. Laid his head on the right side where she always sat, resting on a throw pillow the movers neglected to take, and wished it was her lap. He could almost feel her stroking his hair, like she did after a long gig when he came home exhausted, peeling off sweat and beer-soaked clothes and dropping them in a pile on the bathroom floor, his own music still ringing in his ears, wanting nothing more than silence.

Sometimes she'd hum. It drove him mad—couldn't he have this one thing?

Now, the quiet in the apartment felt permanent, and he'd give anything for that soft humming.

Sleep seemed like it wouldn't come—her face, expressionless, loomed large behind his eyelids—and then it must've, because he blinked and felt like he'd been dreaming, a banal dream of a broken man on an old couch, pretending a throw pillow was everything he'd lost. The clock on the VCR read *three*.

Footsteps padded down the hall.

Mike sat up, throwing off the towels.

"Kara?"

OUR BLACK HEARTS BEAT AS ONE

He went to the hallway—dark, empty, bedroom doors shut. Could she have come back? Realized she'd made a mistake? God, he hoped so—he wouldn't even be angry, he'd take her back with open arms. Maybe they could curl up on the couch, no need for the towels, trade warmth until the sun came up on a new day that would make so much more sense than the last one.

Mike went to her studio door first. Put an ear to the wood and listened.

Skritch, skritch, skritch—soft, like brush strokes on canvas. His pulse quickened at the sound. What if this was all a joke? Or a test? If she did the worst thing she could think of, would he stay, or go out and get drunk and fall into someone else's bed? Mike pushed the door open.

The room was empty.

Moonlight streamed through the window, illuminating pale rectangles on the ground where her desk and cabinet previously sat. The windowsill where she set up her Diamet altar felt conspicuously bare.

"Kara?" he repeated, even though it was stupid, useless.

Then slammed the door on his delusion.

His cheeks reddened. Of course she hadn't come back. The "footsteps" were just the building settling. It made noises incessantly, old bones groaning all night long.

Mike went back to his place on the couch. Shivered the whole night through, without even the illusion of sleep to comfort him, and when the building settled yet again, he caught ahold of his imagination before it took him on another flight of fancy, squeezing tight until he was just a dumb asshole in an old, pre-war apartment with one room too many.

Morning.

A sharp, stabbing pain split his head down the middle.

Mike rubbed his eyes, feeling like he'd fallen headlong into some hedgerhole like the old story. They always said *forever*, him and Kara, the scaffolding on which he'd built his whole future—every dream, every fantasy, every plan— all bound up in her.

How could a forever end?

He realized he'd been sitting on the couch, stewing in his own thoughts, for too long.

Mike went into the kitchen. He usually made coffee, but he didn't want anything. Forced himself to drink a glass of tap water anyway.

He stopped suddenly—the glass was *hers*. Part of him wanted to fling it across the room, smash it against the place on the wall where that damned Condaire painting hung.

Instead, he set it on the counter, carefully, next to the bouquet he never bothered to put in a vase.

What now?

He had work, but couldn't imagine smiling at people, making change, calling their coffee orders over his shoulder. He picked up his phone, started to dial, but tossed it back on the couch instead.

What was the point?

He cast a baleful glance at the throw pillow. A pillow and a glass. A more pathetic summation of their three years together, he couldn't imagine.

But maybe there was more?

He searched the apartment, looking for any traces she might've left behind. Long dark hairs on the sink. An empty shampoo bottle. A coat she never wore in the closet. Refuse, detritus. Useless things she'd shed.

Just like him.

He wished for a note, some secret missive tucked behind the TV or stowed in a shoe. Some explanation for this, what he'd done to earn it. No mere words could fill the yawning, hollow space in his chest.

OUR BLACK HEARTS BEAT AS ONE

At least they'd be something.

Silence was all the apartment had to offer.

Mid-morning, he went out looking for her in the places they used to go—Kimber's Books, Dulcette Park, her favorite pierogi place, even the observation deck at the Cobb Building, where tourists smashed themselves against the railing to get the best angle on the city skyline. Here was where he thought he'd ask her to marry him, when the time came, a thousand feet in the sky. Cheesy, maybe, but you could see the Cobb's spire from anywhere in the city, and he loved the thought of everyone they'd ever known watching when he asked her to join her life to his.

The thought laid him low; he grabbed the railing.

"Are you okay?" a pony-tailed woman asked.

Mike waved her off and lurched across the platform to the elevator. Rode eighty-nine floors down and kept searching.

He went out to "their" house on Cookman, where they went for an open house, once, dressed to the nines and wandering through the hallways of a place they couldn't afford. Assuming the forms of people who could buy that sort of house, trying them on, seeing how it felt. The house sold quickly, but privately they called it *theirs,* and walked by it from time to time to revisit that false future.

Mike stood on the sidewalk, staring at silhouettes in the windows, too thick and angular to ever be theirs.

And walked away.

He wandered for a while. Everywhere he went, insipid couples held hands. He wished he could suck the love right out of their bodies, leave them dry and brittle like himself.

His phone buzzed. Work, probably. Or Donnie and Keegan. He realized he hadn't told anyone yet. Part of him felt like he shouldn't be alone, but the idea of being with someone else seemed too much to bear. He got on the

NDTA for a bit, watched the city pass by, felt the thrum of the wheels rattling on the tracks.

Then got off, waited for another train, and went back the way he came.

Eventually he found a bar he didn't know and drowned himself in pints of Stroman's, shots of Josiah, huddled in a corner away from all the other daytime drunks with their red noses and cigarette-stained hands.

Then someone put Modern Love on the jukebox. Mike whipped around but couldn't tell who it was—maybe the shadow disappearing into the men's room. *Asshole.*

He turned up the collar of his army jacket and staggered out into the grey afternoon. It was drizzling.

Head down, he walked up the street, directionless, just away from the bar.

Wondering if he'd ever walk towards anything again.

That night was worse.

Mike wasn't sure when he ended up back at the apartment. He hadn't drunk enough to black out, but a thick fog filled his mind. Thoughts stumbled over each other, a writhing pile of half-formed ideas struggling for primacy. Television made little sense—beautiful people talking and saying nothing. Fucking and loving nothing. Fighting to achieve nothing.

At some point he must've turned the TV off, because he woke to darkness, a switchblade pressed to his wrist.

He cried out—unintelligible, a potent brew of terror and grief—and dropped the knife. It fell silently to the carpet. He recoiled at the blade's glint in the table lamp, a sickly yellow sheen running down the edge, sickness hiding in every serration.

"Fuck you," Mike said. He kicked the knife across the room, spinning handle-over-blade to disappear under the entertainment center. The dust and spiders had it now.

OUR BLACK HEARTS BEAT AS ONE

He rubbed his face, wishing he could wipe it off completely, reduce his features to a blur and start over, unseen, a pale shape on a street corner. Dragged his fingers down his cheeks, trying to peel his flesh away to find something better, like Dontevolio conjuring the godsduke Xenus from a hunk of marble.

Aside from a stinging redness in his cheeks, his face remained the same as it had always been. Not an unpleasant face, to be sure—simply a face that had been loved, once, and now no longer. Did that make such a face unlovable, or unlovely? How much of the change was him how much Kara? Had he remained static while she sailed off to foreign lands in her mind? Or had he devolved, rotted, the few good parts of him disappearing under her gaze?

He needed out.

Every corner of the apartment was an unquiet ghost, screeching memories. The arm of the couch he'd laid Kara over in better times. The dust outlines marking the appliances she'd taken. Her side of the bedroom, bare, turning the space into a half-completed thought.

All of it said *knife, knife!*

Goddamned if he'd listen. Mike shrugged on his old army jacket and pushed out the door.

He wandered again because that was all he knew. Not in search of Kara this time, but relief from his own thoughts. Down his street, out of the Arts District, into an adjacent neighborhood called the Bellows, home to great ironworks the century previous and nothing now.

Maybe he was looking for the knife again. Throwing himself headlong into the teeth of the night.

He passed beneath bridges, through vacant lots, before lonely stoops where the mean and desperate clustered by burning trash barrels that lent no warmth, like a blur in faded fabric. None remarked on his passing. He left no mark anywhere he trod, leaving Michael Mallory feeling much like a man who'd been snipped clean from existence.

There was an urban legend like that, wasn't there? Far north, in Benoit?

No matter.

After a time, he passed Ehrlich Park—once a viridescent marvel, now further fallen than the Bellows. As a child, he'd played there, when things were better for both of them. Maybe the broken swing, half-buried in dirt, was the same one he'd ridden. The rest of the park was hardly in better condition. The once-proud trees were lightning-scorched or collapsed into deadfall, the iron lampposts toppled. Dead grass had long since blown away, leaving nothing but dust and broken glass.

It seemed a proper place for him.

Maybe Mike could salvage blackened wood from the deadfall, iron from the lampposts. Build a shelter for himself amidst all this decay, and decay with it.

Maybe if he died here, something new would grow. Someday.

He idled down a culvert. Found himself facing a drainage tunnel, tall as he was and half again. A proper place to disappear. Mike stood regarding it, and as he did, in the darkness, four pairs of red eyes opened as one.

He stumbled back, falling on his ass.

"Told you he'd come," a voice said.

"But look what he's brought with him."

"Should we grant him passage, anyway?"

"He won't want to go. Not with that thing in his chest."

Shapes shifted in the dark. A rank, unwashed scent issued forth from the tunnel. "Young man?"

Mike sat frozen on the ground, broken glass biting into his backside. Just a bunch of transients, huddled in a drainage tunnel with their hooch.

So why couldn't he move?

A shuffling sound came from the tunnel. Something neared the mouth, with eight red-shining eyes. Mike expected to see four shuffling men in ratty clothes, paper-bagged bottles clenched tightly in their hands.

But as the eyes neared, something seemed off. They moved as one, a line of four, and each held the other's hand, and their legs looked bound one to the next, like a three-legged race.

Then the clouds shifted, and the moon shone just right, and those hands weren't *held,* they were growing together, like melted plastic—

Mike was up and running before he even realized it. He leapt out of the culvert, heart pounding fiercely, running past the deadfall and out of the park.

Even on the sidewalk, the voices called after him, fainter and fainter but still horribly intelligible.

" . . . *you'll be back . . .* "

" *. . . he'll free us, like Gamoa . . .* "

" *. . . seek her . . .* "

At home, he turned on all the lights and fished the knife out from under the entertainment center.

Not for him, this time.

Mike woke to pounding at the door.

He rolled off the couch. His phone said it was after nine, and he'd missed several more calls. He shoved the phone aside and rubbed his temples.

"Mike? You in there?" a muffled voice called.

Donnie.

Mike groaned and found a pair of pants, shuffled over to the door.

Donnie stood there, all five foot six inches of him—three more with the mohawk—wearing his usual leather jacket, a black Martyrcycle shirt underneath. "Where you been, man?"

"Busy."

"Busy. You look like shit, you're not picking up your

phone. Reina said you missed your shift." Donnie pushed past him into the apartment. "Hey Kara, hope you're decent."

"She's not here." Mike nearly choked on that last word.

Donnie stopped in the middle of the living room, pierced brow arching. Pointed a finger at the wall, the blank rectangles where her pictures used to hang. "You guys painting?"

"No."

Donnie slowly looked around the room. "Holy shit, did she—"

Mike swallowed hard, nodded.

Donnie was across the room in an instant, wrapping his arms around Mike. Wiry, crushing strength.

Mike wanted to shrug him off, but he just stood there, took it. Let Donnie do whatever he felt he needed to.

After a moment, Donnie let him go. Wiped his eyes with his jacket sleeve. He was the emotional one—every show was the best they'd ever played, or utter shit. Keegan was more measured; a long-haired math nerd with box frame glasses. They made a weird couple, but onstage they were totally in sync.

Mike felt something bubbling up inside him. He still hadn't cried. Maybe Donnie was wearing off on him.

"When?" Donnie asked.

"Couple days ago."

"Fuck." Donnie sat on the sofa. "What happened?"

"Wish I knew. Other day, after I left you guys at the Blackwood. Came home and—" he trailed off, unwilling to replay those moments yet again.

"You call her?"

"Phone's off. No idea where she is. If she's in the city, even."

"Maybe she just needs some space," Donnie said. "Clear her head, you know?"

"Maybe." That felt too much like hope. If she needed *space,* whatever that meant, why not just say so?

"You could've called us, you know. We would've been here in a second."

"I know." Thing was, he didn't *want* them, not then, not now. They were good friends—best friends—but they were also a couple. Living reminders of what he'd lost.

Both men fell silent. Donnie didn't seem like he was leaving anytime soon, so Mike dragged a chair over from the dining table and flipped it around, sitting spread-legged. The back of the chair gave him something to lean on. Maybe he should've called somebody, instead of writhing around on the couch. Wandering the city, looking to get hurt or hurt someone else, he still wasn't sure about that part.

The hell had he been doing, anyway? Ehrlich Park? The strange tableau from the drainage pipe came back to him, hands growing into hands, and he shivered.

"What?" Donnie said.

"Nothing."

Donnie tapped his hand on the side of his leg—habit he had if he got off track. Used to do it in school whenever he'd been drawing skulls and demon heads in his notebook and the teacher called on him.

"So, reason I was looking for you. I don't know if you're up for it, but—shit, making you sound like an invalid."

"It's fine."

"Got us a gig tomorrow. The Beacon."

"That's good." The Beacon was an old, converted theater on the north side. Thousand-head capacity. Modern Love usually packed it to the rafters.

"That's not all. This A&R guy from TRG/Anti-Scope's going to be there."

Mike gaped at him. "No shit?"

"Guess they finally listened to all those tapes we've been sending."

TRG/Anti-Scope. The big boys. Mike could barely believe it.

Donnie pushed himself off the couch. "You want to grab a drink, work out the set list? You know Keegs doesn't give a shit as long as we play "Liminal Gods" and anything with a weird-ass time signature."

Mike caught the blank rectangle where the Condaire print used to hang out of the corner of his eye. "Maybe later."

"Come on, you just going to sit around the apartment?"

Mike didn't say anything.

"Yeah, okay." Donnie headed for the door. "Practice later though?"

"Sure."

Donnie was halfway down the hall before Mike figured he should've said *thanks for coming by*.

Instead, he locked the door, sat back down on the couch, head in his hands, wishing he could get excited for something he'd wanted all his life.

Mike pulled out the acoustic, tried to work through a few standards—"Liminal Gods," "Drunk on Nothing," "Heads Are Gonna Roll." But his hands shook, his voice cracked with every note.

Shit luck. Couldn't good things have waited a respectable amount of time before so rudely deciding to happen to him? Shouldn't the universe know he could bear more misfortune, wounded as he was, but anything wonderful would be wasted?

He gripped the neck of the guitar so tight his hands hurt, cocked it back, ready to bash it into the wall—

A door creaked in the hallway.

Mike frowned—the damned pre-war building settling itself was enough to snap his rage like a rubber band. He laid the guitar carefully down on the couch, sickened by his own anger.

"Damn it, Kara," Mike muttered, like he'd done a hundred or a thousand or a million times already.

Never damning *her,* per se. Just the thing that had grown between them, unnoticed, expanding and pushing them away, so divorced from each other they might've been shunted off into separate universes.

Something Kara used to say when they fought— *Sometimes I think we're on different sides of the stars.*

Maybe he should've believed her.

Creak.

The door again. Maybe he hadn't latched it. Mike ran a hand along the acoustic's wooden body—*sorry for what I almost did*—and stepped into the hall.

Kara's office door was ajar. He wondered how long he'd call it that, before it became something else.

If he stayed, even.

Mike went to push the door closed but opened it instead—maybe wanting to hurt again, let the emptiness smash into him over and over until there was nothing left.

No emptiness—her desk, covered in brushes and paint; her easel, with a fresh canvas. The windowsill, filled with stubby, half-burnt candles, a tantagram-emblazoned celeman cloth, a strip of flypaper clotted with tiny, dead, black bodies.

Diamet.

Mike blinked. Her room, empty again. Momentarily filled by his cruel imagination. Wasn't enough for Kara to hurt him like she had, his mind had to get in on the action, too—

The closet door stood open.

Odd, it hadn't been open the night before, when he'd imagined footsteps in the hall.

"Hello?"

His voice echoed in the small space, answering his question. The only answer he'd ever have.

He crossed to the closet door. Maybe it hadn't been latched, either, and the ever-settling building dislodged it. Or maybe she'd come back, creeping in while he was off peering into drainage pipes and indulging insane visions of hands melting together, to get something she'd forgotten. Just because he could find vanishingly few of her things didn't mean they weren't there. Sharing a home, possessions seep into the spaces, hide in plain sight. Impossible to truly extricate her life from his in the span of hours.

Mike looked in the closet—empty. He went to push the door closed.

Wait.

Something on the top shelf. He went back to the kitchen for a chair.

The chair wobbled when he stood on it. For the briefest moment, he pictured himself falling, cracking his head on the floor. Not enough height to end his agony, but the thought of exploring a different kind of pain thrilled him. Maybe he wasn't meant to feel better, but to find new ways to hurt.

What he should be looking for.

Mike steadied himself, then inspected the top shelf. A dark, rectangular object was pushed up against the wall, bathed in shadow. He pulled it to himself—leathery, rough—and dragged it into the light.

A book.

Old, musty, nothing he'd heard of. A faded tantagram stamped into the cover. He ran his fingers over the grooves.

" . . . *seek her* . . . "

A shiver ran through him. He glanced over his shoulder instinctively.

Nothing.

He took the book back into the living room. Flipped on a table lamp, bathing the room in a yellow glow. The book was hers, no doubt. Kara had always been obsessed with magic, witchcraft. Her Diamet altars were just the start. Such beliefs had often been a point of tension in their relationship. When they'd first moved in together, he'd been hanging pictures when a sour smell assailed him. Followed it to her studio, where she sat cross-legged on the floor, chanting and burning danderwort.

"At least open a window," Mike said.

Kara pushed the door shut in his face. "Next time, knock."

He didn't mind the altars, or the murmured prayers. And he definitely didn't mind the *look*—black lace and silver jewelry, deep eyeshadow. Modern Love was often described as goth-adjacent, since Mike's lyrics conjured up visions of mausoleums, restless dead, black wings beating against the window. But while Mike found the superficialities of the supernatural unendingly compelling, he didn't actually *believe* in it. His interests in esotericism went no further than the peculiar magic a few choice chords could work on the right audience.

Now, sitting on the couch with some strange grimoire in his lap, he wanted to believe more than anything.

Maybe Kara was right, there was something more to this world than atoms and elements, some hidden grand design just waiting to be uncovered by the right ritual.

If there was, couldn't he follow the path she walked, and if he did—

Would it lead him to her?

Hearts break. But they don't *just* break, they explode.

Destroying everything around them.

The old Michael Mallory never would've given the old book a second thought. But he died the second Kara uttered three terrible words—*it's not working.*

This new Michael Mallory opened the book and began to read.

The leather-bound volume seemed like it was written in high Terrine at first, a dead language Mike recognized from bygone classics classes, but after flipping through a few pages, the words resolved themselves into a familiar tongue. The purpose of the volume soon became clear.

It was a book of spells.

Mike ran his fingers over the pages, marveling at how Kara must've done the same. The first spell that stopped him was a love spell. He read over the ingredients, all minor items he could scavenge from the apartment—hair, a glass or bottle, etc.

If he wanted to, he could cast this very spell.

Conspiracies blossomed—what if this was her plan? Some test? Why not leave, but give him a way to follow, if only he could cast aside his rationality for a moment?

What did he love more, her or himself? Or at least the piece of himself that scoffed whenever she set up her Diamet altar, burned danderwort, and drew ornate symbols all over her body in daum, writhing in candlelight to a soundless music that touched her more deeply than Mike's own songs ever could? What if *that* was the reason he'd been looking for, and if he could excise his doubt, his skepticism, she'd come back through that door, the movers behind her, grunting and straining up four flights of stairs, and everything would be set right?

No.

Maybe she wanted him to find this book, explore the world she lived in and he mocked. But a love spell, even if successfully cast, would always be a lie. A shadow of the feelings they shared—

Once shared.

Mike turned the page.

The rest of the book was useless—long, impenetrable treatises on subjects so esoteric he couldn't make head nor tails of what they even purported to describe.

A sudden sob wracked him, he dropped the book on the carpet. An unseen weight crushed his chest, pinning his heart against his ribcage. He felt sick. Mike laid a hand on his chest—cold, clammy—and wished he could rip that diseased organ out, carry it to the garbage chute, let it fall, unwanted, like a plastic-bound bag of kitchen refuse.

His heart—

Fuck love spells. What he really needed was an anti-love spell. Some hex to make him forget how badly he hurt.

Something Kara said once came back to him, another time he'd interrupted her in her studio. Cross-legged, thumbs pressed against middle fingers, sitting in a tantagram drawn on the floor in chalk and surrounded by burning candles.

"There's a spell for everything. But some, nobody's bothered to write down. When that happens—" her dusky, mascara-shrouded eyes bored into his own, "—you've got to make your own kind of magic."

He didn't believe her, not in the way she meant, but he liked the turn of phrase, centering a whole song around it; "Egomancy."

Some old book couldn't help him, but maybe he could tap into the power it promised, all the same. Mike got the acoustic, laid it across his lap. Still in tune, despite the violence he'd threatened earlier.

"You're a good old gal," he said, patting her, then sang:

> *If the grimoire's blank*
> *Make your own kind of magic.*

He lost himself in the song, or found himself, and the weight on his chest lessened. Still there, an invisible hand pushing on his breast, but weaker and less insistent. He leaned back, closed his eyes—

And let the visions come.

Pages in a book of his own, spelling out exactly what he needed to do, the flowery script outlining a path forward that had nothing to do with finding Kara, compelling her to love him again.

And everything to do with saving his own life.

How he ended up at a butcher shop five minutes before closing, and why he now mounted the steps to their apartment—no, *his* apartment—with a hunk of bloody muscle wrapped in butcher paper.

Rounded the corner—Donnie and Keegan were waiting for him. Donnie's mohawk looked a little limper from the morning. He sucked a can of Stroman's in a brown bag.

Keegan leaned against the wall, skinny arms crossed over his babybird chest, long black hair framing his face. He rarely took anything stronger than a Big and Jake's. The music was his drug.

"Uh, hey," Mike said.

"What's that?" Donnie asked.

Mike looked at the package in his hands, like he was surprised to find himself holding anything. "Dinner."

Keegan rolled his eyes, vegetarian sensibilities minorly offended by the brown drippings seeping through the butcher paper.

"Whatever," Donnie said. "Not picking up your phone again, I see."

"Sorry."

"Only the biggest show of our whole damn career tomorrow and here you are, grocery shopping. What happened to practice?"

"Can we get one in tomorrow?"

Keegan shook his head. "Work. All day."

"Look, we've played these songs a million times. We'll kill it."

Donnie said, "Or maybe we'll fuck it all up because your head's not right."

Keegan squeezed his arm. "Easy."

Mike didn't want *easy*. Wasn't fair to everyone else. Shit happened, it was called being a professional.

The weight hit him again. He nearly dropped the pig's heart.

"Look," Donnie said. "It hurts, I've been there."

Keegan shifted uncomfortably. Donnie was the only person he'd ever dated.

"But you gotta push past it. For a night. Because if you don't, whenever you come out of this—"

"And you will come out of this," Keegan leaned forward to say.

"—you'll regret it if you don't give the show your all."

They were right, even if he couldn't imagine getting up on stage and singing songs about falling in and out of love in a dark, phantom-haunted city by the sea.

Not with this heart.

"Let's go out," Donnie said. "We'll make it an early one, but—"

"It's okay," Mike said, holding up the pig's heart. "Dinner."

"Fine. I'll have one for you."

"Just one," Keegan said. "You play like crap when you're hungover."

"Pssh," Donnie said, ambling down the hall. "I'm a professional."

What's in a spell?

It's like a name, a descriptor of something that already exists. Say a man's name to curse him or call him. Say a spell's name to put it into action.

The universe's mysteries are simple at heart. We lend them complexity, because to understand everything that ever was or could be would bring a madness beyond functioning. If God exists, he sleeps, because not even a superintellect could bear the knowledge it contained all potentiality. Such cognition accuses and damns—why are your infinite somethings superior to infinite nothing, Tonans?

God could never live with himself.

Mike sat at the dining table, unwrapping the pig's

heart, wondering if this might stave off his burgeoning madness, or call it forth into the light. The rest of the apartment was dark, but for a few candles throwing shadows on the wall. He tried not to look, because when he did, his mind turned them into things they couldn't be.

Meat juice ran slick through the furrows of the paper, spilling onto the table. He wiped it off with a kitchen towel, thinking he should've put newspaper down, but by then it was too late. The only thing left was to do the thing he planned, the thing that came to him while he strummed "Egomancy" in the empty apartment.

By the sink, the wine bottle waited, the same one Kara had opened the day she broke it off. Flies clotted the bottle's throat. Mike dumped it in the sink and smashed the bottle against the counter.

It broke, showering his boots with shards of dark glass. His hand shook, grasping the broken neck. He kicked the glass into a little pile and returned to the table.

Where the heart waited.

Candles guttered at his approach. The room stank of blood, a thick, cloying coppery smell. He inhaled deeply. Scent was particulate. Every huff of bloodstench made the heart a part of him.

And hopefully, he of it.

Mike took a deep breath and uttered strange words, hoping they'd form some sort of enticing appeal for anything that might be listening. The refrain had come to him from nothing, and now he repeated them, sung instead of spoken, because even when the world made no sense at all, Michael Mallory knew where his true power lay:

"Monahem, Aloischem, Argonem, acolytes of Gamoa the Severed, vestige of Raquine. Bear witness to my preparations. Let this be my organ," he placed a hand on the pig's heart, shivering at the slimy, cold texture, "and let this poor organ die by my hand."

OUR BLACK HEARTS BEAT AS ONE

He raised the broken wine bottle high above the heart—

And pierced it through.

Mike stepped back from the table, chest heaving. The wine bottle stuck upright in the bleeding heart, like a standard on a battlefield.

God, how he hoped he'd conquered.

The Tin Bard

THE TIN BARD

MIKE WOKE UP on the couch. His hands were covered in sticky reddish streaks. He'd passed out without even washing up, apparently. He didn't remember falling asleep. The last thing he remembered was the heart, pierced through, and a great thrumming pressure building in his eardrums. The world slipping away.

A sign it worked? Or just further evidence of his decline?

He didn't feel any different. He'd expected everything to change, completely and irrevocably. Foolish. Magic was no more real than the years he'd shared with Kara.

They were false, weren't they? If she could leave like that, no discussion? Disappear herself from his life?

She never really loved him.

Mike's hands went to his face in anticipation of a sob that never came. He stared at the ceiling for far too long— off-white, bland. Pushed himself up.

The clock below the TV read three in the afternoon.

"Shit." Mike looked around for his phone, found it on the counter. Several missed texts from Donnie and Keegan both.

"I'm fine. Be there for sound check," he replied without bothering to read any of the messages. He needed to shower, grab his guitar, and make his way cross-town on the NDTA. Some bands had pre-show rituals—the guys from Backstroke always ate at the same pierogi place, while

27

Tom Sadler from Hartsbane drew hash marks on his forearms in magic marker for reasons he never explained to anyone. You could tell how good a Hartsbane show was from how smudged his arms were for the encore.

Mike and the guys were too rational for that shit, so he had some time. He cleaned up, chucking the pig's heart down the garbage chute, along with Kara's old book. What the hell did he need that thing for?

He left the broken wine bottle on the table. Not because it was a thing of Kara's—he liked the way it looked in the middle of the table, like a murderous game of spin-the-bottle had been played.

He took his time showering, scrubbing blood from his hands. Had he even showered since Kara left? He couldn't remember.

Pathetic. Spiraling like that over *one* chick, when he was *the* Michael Mallory? He could fuck practically any girl with a septum piercing in the whole goddamn city. In front of their boyfriends, even.

Once he'd washed the death off of him, Mike stood in front of the mirror, spiking his short, blonde hair. Went in the bedroom, pulled on a black sleeveless t-shirt— Martyrcycle, same as Donnie wore the day before—and jeans, capping the outfit off with steel-toed Calibers and his usual army jacket. Checked himself in the mirror again—

Damn.

Actually looked like himself again. He even wore a half-smile that was making a credible threat to turn into a real one. Mike sneered—*the hell was wrong with you, man*?

She did you a favor.

Mike opened his closet and picked out a guitar— Kristofferson Electric. He usually went with his High Diamond and its simple black body. But hell, he was in the mood.

He grabbed his phone—nearly charged—and sent Donnie and Keegs another text.

OUR BLACK HEARTS BEAT AS ONE

Drinks before?

Two thumbs-up glyphs came back, rapid-fire.

Mike checked his hair one last time and headed out the door.

"What the fuck was that?"

They were in the green room, post-show, sweat-drenched. Donnie sat on an amp wearing a beer somebody chucked at him during "Crimson Crush." Keegan still held his drumsticks, spinning them around, gripping them so hard his knuckles went white.

Mike stood by the door, guitar case slung over his shoulders. "What do you mean, *what the fuck?*"

Donnie rose, hands bunching into fists. "I literally mean what the fuck was that out there, Mike?"

"I was perfect. Hit every single note."

"Yeah, you did. Technically perfect. But god, man, you were, were—"

"Hollow," Keegan chimed in.

"Hollow," Donnie repeated, wagging a finger at Mike. "That's it. Like you didn't, like, *feel* anything."

"Okay, you really want to recap?" Mike said. "Let's talk about your backing vocals on 'Best We Leave.'"

"*My* backing vocals?"

"Best *we* leave," Mike sang. "You know what a *G* is?"

"Yeah?"

"This is you." Mike sang the lyrics again, voice cracking on *we*. "And you're the one giving me shit?"

"I made one mistake, okay? But you—fuck!" Donnie spun and kicked the amp.

"Easy," Keegan said, squeezing his arm. "You don't know that A&R guy—"

"Oh, I fucking know," Donnie said. "Hope you like grinding it out at local shows, maybe stringing together enough for a regional tour, and motherfucker I hope you

29

like your day job—oh wait, you quit—well I hope you like starving then, because you just fucked us!"

"*Us*? I'm the band. You're just the rhythm section."

The color drained from Donnie's face. Keegan looked away, fiddling with his drumsticks.

"Okay, first of all, blow me," Donnie said. "I write songs."

"Right, like 'Sweet Lianna.' That's the one everybody's screaming for at encore, yeah? Oh wait, it's a glorified B-side. This whole crowd—" Mike motioned in the direction of the venue, where everybody was filing out or getting into last-minute fistfights, "—is here for me, not you two assholes. They—"

"Assholes, huh?" Keegan said, flipping the hair out of his face. He shoved his drumsticks in his pocket and walked out the door.

"Real nice," Donnie said, scowling at Mike. "You're a fucking dick." He hurried after Keegan.

Mike shook his head. Ingrates. All they had to do was keep time, sing backup. Hell, Keegan only had a job because Static Ghost was already the drum machine band in ND, and no scene would put up with more than one of those. And basically anybody could play bass, half the crowd could probably do a passable job. Honestly, he'd been carrying them both for longer than he cared to admit. He was the genius, the idol. They were—

"Umm, hey," a voice behind him said.

Mike turned, instantly placing the green-haired girl with the shredded fishnets in front of him—front row, singing along to every word. Locked eyes with him more than once, most notably during "Bones of the City," when she licked the air lasciviously.

"Hey," Mike said. "Who let you back here?"

She shrugged. "No one."

"A rebel. I like that." He pulled her towards him by the hips.

She was already turning her lips up to meet his.

OUR BLACK HEARTS BEAT AS ONE

They stood on the sidewalk, the Beacon dark behind them. Some bartender had caught them fucking on the old leather couch in the green room. Ordinarily, Mike would've been pissed at the interruption, but he didn't really care and neither did the green-haired girl whose name he hadn't bothered with. The second their clothes came off he knew his heart wasn't in it, and her eyes said the same, but the both of them went through with it anyway, her for the story—*can you believe who I fucked*—and him for no reason at all.

"You want to get some food?" Mike said, not meaning it.

The girl held up her phone. "I would, but I just called a Koach. Got work, you know?"

Mike should've called one himself—the NDTA stopped running at 1am—but he was still hyped from the show, the argument with the two assholes, getting his dick wet. The night needed to continue, even if Green-Hair wasn't in his plans—

"What the fuck," Mike said.

"Huh?"

Across the street, a girl was walking alone, head down, wearing a hoodie. He couldn't see her face, but he was sure it was Kara. He knew her gait, the way she held herself. Once he spotted her in front of a honey stand at the Truxton Market from fifty feet away.

"Uh, goodnight, I guess," Green-Hair said to his back, because Mike was already halfway across the street.

He'd left his Kristofferson in the green room, but it would keep. He wondered why she was here, if she even knew he was playing, or if she'd somehow wended her way here for another reason altogether—some universal force, gravitational, magnetic, pulling them back together?

He wanted to call out to her, but he didn't, fearful that might drive her away.

Instead, he followed.

Through dark and silent streets, past empty storefronts and construction sites. Outside a newer apartment building, a woman stood on a grass patch with her dog and remarked not at all on Kara's passing, but turned to stare at him coming thirty feet later, her eyes boring into his, and then the dog looked too, back arched as it voided its bowels into the grass.

"Hi," he said, waving.

The dog growled.

Then the woman did too, teeth clenched, eyes bulging in her skull.

He turned up his collar and hurried on.

Cold, but not as cold as he'd been these last few days. Kara walked on, head down, never looking behind her. He practiced what he'd say if she did, wondered what he'd do if she didn't, if she suddenly bounded up the steps of some brownstone, disappearing behind a security door into whatever new life she'd made for herself.

Part of him knew how fucked up this was. Stalkerish. He caught a glimpse of himself in a dirty rain puddle and looked away.

Unable to bear what might be looking back at him.

They walked for hours. Days. Years. More time than they'd had together. Past high rises and townhouses, vacant lots and shuttered stores. Cracked and broken streets.

A woman and her shade.

Trashcan fires bloomed on the sidewalks. Somehow, they'd entered the Bellows. Kara walked past shadow-men huddling together for warmth. If they noticed her, they didn't acknowledge it.

When Mike passed, they looked upon him, and just as swiftly looked away.

What the hell was she doing down here? How had they strayed so far from the cozy, fourth-floor walk-up they'd called home? How could they walk so far together, and yet apart?

Kara stepped off the sidewalk into Ehrlich Park.

Mike stopped short, watching her meander down a path into the trees. Passing strange she'd come here, to the same place his shattered heart drew him. Yet it gave him hope— whatever unknown distance had opened up between them, something still tethered them. Seeking the same thing, or each equally lost, but nodding to the same rhythm.

Perhaps, perhaps.

He took a deep breath and entered the park.

The dead trees encircled. Lampposts flickered, their dull light a mere suggestion. Kara became one with the shadows. He followed her sounds. Her boots crunched gravel and broken glass.

Mike left the trail, taking to the grass, where he could walk without alerting her. Up ahead, the trees receded. He saw her shadow once again.

Slipping down into the drainage culvert.

He nearly let out a scream, thinking of the tunnel and the strange thing he'd seen within, but stopped himself. A vision, conjured up by his confused, sleepless, battered mind. Maybe the drunks he'd seen still lingered in the tunnel, but they were only that.

If there were men in that tunnel, and they meant her harm, he'd intervene.

Maybe that would be enough.

Kara paused before the tunnel, glancing back over her shoulder, her face shrouded by the hood. After an eternity, she looked away.

And entered the tunnel.

One second, she was there, the next she was gone, as if she'd blinked out of existence. Mike pictured dirty hands grabbing her, pulling her into their subterranean world with grim finality.

He ran.

BRIAN ASMAN

"Kara!" he yelled, done with stealth. "Wait!"

She did not reemerge.

Mike came to a stop just outside the tunnel. Peered inside. "Kara?"

Eight flames flickered in the dark. Four sets of eyes.

Every one upon him.

A shuffling sound came from the tunnel and a rancid stench. Blood, unwashed bodies.

"He's back."

"And he's lost the little thing that blocked his way."

The sound came closer. Mike's hands shook.

"Let her go!" Mike called, cursing the quaver in his voice. "I'm warning you."

A dry chuckle came from the tunnel. "Warning us?"

"If only we'd been warned."

"Too little—"

"—too late."

And then the thing in the tunnel reached the mouth, blocking the passage. Moonlight shone down, showing it for what it was.

Men.

Four in a line—filthy, disheveled—wearing threadbare suits. Each held the other's hand so tightly they appeared intertwined, except one on the end bled freely from shorn skin. Their trousers twisted around the legs of their fellows, like they'd come from an eight-legged race. Some silly, exaggerated picnic game played once upon a time.

"What the hell are you?"

One man smiled, showing a handful of mossy green teeth. "We are Rat King."

Mike's heart pounded faster. "Where is she? What did you do to her?"

The men on either end spoke as one. "Who?"

"Kara!"

"We know no Kara."

"No, she was just—"

"No one is here but you. Did you come to join us?"

"No, I—"

All four laughed.

One of the middlemen said, "A jest, that's all. You can't join us, we're already joined. See?" He nodded to his right.

Their hands—they weren't *holding* hands. Their flesh, four different hues, had grown together, fingers leeching into knuckles. Even the hairs on their fingers twined, tying together like shoelaces.

Mike's stomach lurched.

"How easy it is to forget," an endsman said.

"That all the world isn't like us," the other bookend completed.

"Or are they?" a middleman said. "And we're just honest about it?"

"Honest ones!" all four said.

"Better than *Rat King*."

"Maybe they shouldn't hide their bonds."

"With words like family, friend."

Mike careened between revulsion and anger. "Move aside. I have to find—"

"You hear that?" a middleman said to the others.

"Best listen," a bookend said.

"He has no bonds. Cut them all away, he has."

"And yet he's seeking. Foolish."

The men held up their fused hands again. "Shear our bonds, like you've shorn your own. Then you may pass."

Mike pictured his knife slicing between fingers and knuckles, cutting through the webbing, blood running down entwined palms.

For a moment, he thought he could do it.

If he had it.

An endsman laughed. "Kidding."

"Someone could cut us apart, but not you."

As one, the four men shuffle-stepped to the side, pressing their bodies against the wall of the tunnel.

"Go," a middleman said. "But remember."

"You can only go this way twice."

"Once for love. Once for hate."

The four men bent their chins to their chests.

Then they faded into the shadows.

Gone. Before he could utter another word.

Just like Kara.

Their scent lingered—musky, rancid—and then that was gone too, leaving Mike wondering again. Some cruel trick, played by a sleep-starved mind. Hands didn't do that. He leaned heavily against the tunnel wall and rubbed his face. If he'd imagined the men—

—*Rat King*—

Then couldn't he have imagined Kara? Not just now, but then too? Living in a pre-war walk-up, restoring a vintage Vechno-Conquest motorcycle, humming melodies to himself while he made lattes, writing songs the whole damn city fought and fucked to. Maybe that was the dream, and this, *this* was reality.

Roaming cracked and barren streets in an old army jacket. Shivering in the rain. Unknown and unseen but for the snarling of dogs and sideways glances tossed his way by the people he haunted.

"Fuck," Mike muttered. He looked back at the drainage ditch. He could go back the way he came, into Ehrlich Park, then the Bellows. Find a trashcan fire to warm himself, some sunken faces and sullen eyes for company. Drink rotgut liquor until he became real again—sickeningly, head-poundingly real—or passed from this world entirely.

Then again, he'd come this far.

Mike pulled out his phone, used the paltry light to scan the tunnel. Dark things skittered into the shadows. At his feet—broken glass, a stream of dirty water, a rusting wheel adorned with the rotting rubber remnants of a tire.

And darkness, as far as he could see.

And then, up ahead—the faintest pinprick of light, a

fleeting luminescence oh-so-briefly in conversation with his own.

Again—"Kara?" His voice echoed down the empty tunnel.

And was not answered.

Then he was running, boots splashing in dirty water, dodging abandoned hunks of metals, scraps of wood, piles of rat droppings, chasing that ephemeral promise of light. Of *her*.

All tunnels have an end, don't they? That's the agreement.

Every passage leads somewhere.

And then he felt a great rush of wind, a flash of light. He stopped short, found himself standing at the other end of the tunnel, looking out on a river. Above, an old steel bridge.

The rain came with a force that threatened it might never stop. He turned up his collar and wandered into this new and strange part of the city, boots clicking on cobblestones until he found somewhere to go.

The Proluxian.

That's what the neon screamed, blazing purple letters twining each other like undulating snakes.

Or hands growing into each other.

Half-remembered classical lessons came back to him— the giant Prolux, slaying the silent god Jinghara so that men could talk to each other. The sign in the dusty, smoked windows said *Open,* but the door wouldn't budge. Maybe they forgot the sign.

Except he could see shadows moving beyond that smoked glass.

A groaning door opened in the side alley, letting out a quick burst of chatter and music. Mike stepped into the alley. He gave as wide a berth as he could to the overflowing trashcans, crushing crumpled wrappers under his feet. An iron door was set into the side of the building. Despite the refuse and the general condition of the neighborhood, the setup shouted private, exclusive. He'd been in places like this before, dragged along by the hangers-on that clung around the edges of the music scene, trading access and drugs for a chance to be seen. Odds were, anybody on the door would know *him*. After all, he was Michael fucking Mallory of Modern Love.

Or at least the shade of such.

Mike pounded on the door—wincing at his fist striking metal—then stuck his hands in the pockets of his army jacket, like he didn't give a shit if they let him in or not.

A peephole in the door squeaked open, then slammed shut. The door opened inward, offering another burst of shouting voices and music, with bodies writhing in the relative darkness, booze and bodyspray and something else—fresh mud?—wafting out.

Mike shot a last glance down the alley and stepped inside.

The room was cavernous and dark, lit by wall sconces. Something unfamiliar and electronic blared from the speakers, a mass of indistinct dancers filling the middle of the room, some with glow sticks circled around their necks, most wearing little more.

"ID?" a voice at his shoulder said.

Mike yelped, turned towards the speaker. A girl sat on a vinyl stool—long, blonde hair held back with batwing barrettes, heavy eyeshadow, wearing a leather jacket and tight black skirt underneath, and a silver chain at her throat. She held her hand out.

"Uh, yeah," Mike shouted over the noise. Nobody ever asked him for ID. He fished his beaten, brown leather wallet from his pocket and handed it over.

The girl peered carefully at the ID, to him, back again.

"On my right is Michael," she said, smirking, except

she pronounced his name *Mick-a-ail* instead of *My-call*. She pressed the card back into his hand. "She's downstairs. I'll take you."

"Kara?"

But the girl was already pushing her way onto the dance floor.

Mike followed.

The dancers parted for her like ocean waves in a fable. Just enough to allow passage. Mike brushed shoulders with a few of them, who pirouetted away at his touch.

On the other side of the dance floor, more patrons crowded the bar. A man in a Tandsfield hat and a woman draped in feathers fucked openly against the wall. A woman with a half-shaved head and tattoos all over her face turned towards him, raised her glass—a crystal decanter, brimming with a dark liquid.

To the right of the crowded bar was a door. The girl opened it, looked over her shoulder—maybe to ensure Mike was still behind her—and for a moment, their eyes met. Hers were grey, like his. A jolt of electricity went through Mike's body, his stomach clenched.

Then he looked away.

"Coming?"

Mike followed her into a stairwell. Wooden stairs curved off to the right. The door shut behind him and the music abruptly cut off.

The stairs were wide enough for them to walk side-by-side, and brightly lit compared to the rest of the club by overhead sodium lights. They descended to the landing, turned right, then down another set of stairs.

Mike shot a sidelong glance at the girl, who was chewing her lower lip, the memory of the current that rushed through him when their eyes met—so much like an actual feeling—still fresh. "You don't look like a bouncer."

And immediately kicked himself for saying something so stupid.

The girl stopped suddenly. "And you don't look like a husk. But here you are anyway."

"I—"

She snorted. "It's fine. I get that all the time."

"Really?"

"No. But it's okay."

"Thanks." Mike looked down at his boots. "What'd you mean? A husk?"

"Just because I forgive you doesn't mean I'm explaining anything. Now come."

She skipped down the stairs. Mike hurried to follow her. She reached the bottom first and spun around.

"In there," the girl said, pointing at yet another door.

Mike swallowed. *Kara.* He'd yearned for this, desperate to feel the warmth of her body, breathe in the scent of her hair, one more time. Dreaming he could die in that moment, so the last thing he knew in this world would be the only thing that ever really mattered to him.

But here he was, and his heart didn't pound, his palms didn't clam up. His butterflies lay still in his stomach, a pile of dried wings flaking into nothingness.

Curious, surely. To hear what she had to say, and show her what had become of him—

—a husk—

—this scarecrow in an Army jacket, dick covered in the juices of a girl he'd never wanted and who hadn't wanted *him* once she had him. A shadow, sundered from the form that cast it, untethered and blown about without purpose. The echo of a note, still resounding, but unable to do anything but diminish, diminish, shrinking into a memory of itself.

The girl grabbed his wrist, gave it a squeeze. "I can't open the door for you. If you can live with yourself, come upstairs. I'll even buy you a drink. And then when the music stops, I'll turn you out into the morning with the rest of them. You won't find your way home, but you'll find your way somewhere."

OUR BLACK HEARTS BEAT AS ONE

She turned to him, gazing up into his eyes. Mike felt no spark of electricity, but the memory of such, and it pained him.

"If you seek her again, she'll be gone. You can look forever. Trawl desperate and dismal places. Truck with beggars and kings. You'll only go mad for the searching. I could tell you tales of men and women who've done the same. But it wouldn't matter. You've lived them."

She let go of his wrist and made for the stairs.

"Open the door. Or don't. I can't tell you if you should. Only what it costs."

He ignored that. "Why do you care?"

The girl touched the chain around her neck. "I had my own door, once. I didn't open it." She hurried off, dematerializing to nothing more than clomping boots in the stairwell.

Leaving him alone with the door.

He ran his fingers down the wood, flush with the grain. Leaned an ear against it. Throbbing music pulsed through the bones of the old building. Was she really waiting for him on the other side?

Did it even matter?

Mike reached down and turned the knob before he could stop himself. The door swung inward, revealing a dim, candlelit room. A simple wooden table to his right, covered with melting candles. Directly opposite, a bank of box fans of all shapes and sizes stacked one atop the other formed something of a wall, bisecting the room down the middle and throwing light in rhythmic slashes across the walls. The breeze they brought washed over him, fresh and cool and smelling of redagalias from the Truxton market.

A shape moved behind the fans. Pacing. Obscured by the whirling blades.

"Kara?"

At the sound of her name, the shape stopped.

Mike rushed forward, getting as close as he could. He

grasped a fan by its plastic frame, ready to toss it aside, to see *her* again, to—

"Stop." The voice was deep and old and sounded nothing like Kara. "Disturb nothing in this room."

Mike held up his hands. "I thought you were her. Where's Kara?"

"I don't know anyone by that name."

"Then who are you?"

The fans churned, the visage beyond them inscrutable. "What do you want?"

Fan air feathered his hair. He closed his eyes and tried to feel anything.

"Do you want things to be like they are?"

"No."

"Do you want things to be like they were?"

Day before, he would've said yes. But now the very concept of wanting things seemed academic. He understood the idea of going back, before he came home and found Kara in the kitchen, a wineglass on the counter and words he couldn't begin to understand on her lips. And maybe this strange woman waiting behind the bank of fans could grant it. The world wasn't what he thought it was. The Rat King showed him that.

But if she did, wouldn't that be just like the love spells in Kara's book? A version of it?

A love compelled is no love at all.

"Not like they were," he finally said. "But not like this."

The woman was silent for a time, then said, "You cut out your heart."

"I didn't know it would work."

"Magic is powerful. Especially if you don't know what you're doing. And this close to Diamet."

The word echoed in the room, to the beat of the whirling fans—*Diamet, Diamet, Diamet.*

"Do you want your heart back?"

Mike squeezed his eyes shut. Behind them, scales—one

weighed down with the pain he'd felt since Kara left, a seeping hunk of blackened flesh still pulsing with tumorous life; the other filled with Donnie and Keegs and the girl he hadn't wanted, their skin sparkling like gold.

A song he hadn't written yet played in his mind. Better than "Liminal Gods," better than "Drunk On Nothing." The sort of song that would echo on down through the ages long after he was rotting in his coffin, reduced to dry yellow bones, then powder, atoms, nothing.

" . . . Black hearts . . . "

You'll write that, a voice whispered. *If you choose wisely.*

"I want it back," Mike said. "But not like before. Better."

All the fans stopped at once. Blades and shadow still obscured the woman's face, but her skin stretched in something like a smile. "Your old heart is gone. But I can make you another. If you're willing to work for it."

"How?"

"There's a tape recorder on the table."

Mike shot a look over his shoulder—there it was, beneath a wax-dripping candelabra. "What do I do?"

"Bring me three stories. A love won, a love lost, a love avenged. With those, I'll forge a new heart. Superior to what you've known."

"How do I do that?"

"Just get them to talk. Take Evangeline, she'll help you."

"Who's—"

"The one who brought you here. She's waiting upstairs."

Mike wanted to ask her more questions, but he couldn't think of anything to say. It sounded absurd, infinitely crazier than the metaphysical arguments that had fractured his relationship with Kara.

But he wasn't that man anymore. So why the fuck not?

"Okay," he said, picking up the tape recorder and putting it to his lips. He hummed a few bars of the song he'd heard when he closed his eyes, the song of the scales, the song he'd someday write when he had a heart again.

Then it left him.

The fans whirled to life. "Go," the woman said.

Mike slipped the tape recorder into the pocket of his army jacket and stepped out of the room. The door slammed shut behind him. He mounted the stairs, a tremor in his hand. He could barely swallow. When he came back out into the club above, the room was empty, the floor littered with crumpled napkins and glow sticks and feather boas.

How long had he been down there?

"Thanks, asshole," a voice to his right said.

Mike turned.

Evangeline stood behind the bar, holding a bottle of Josiah. She took it back, the kind of bolt that would lay a grown man low. She wiped the back of her mouth with her sleeve.

Then threw the bottle at him.

Evangeline leaned over him, pressing a bar rag, fattened with ice, to his head. The house lights blazed, too bright.

He groaned, tried to sit up.

"Don't move," Evangeline said. "You hit your head."

"You hit *my* head."

"Says the guy with the head injury."

"Fine." Arguing only made his head hurt worse.

"I'm not going to say sorry, because I don't believe in lying to people you don't give a shit about. But I will say it's *her* fault, not yours, and I'm so—" she turned to the stairwell and raised her voice, "—fucking *sick* of this. Not enough I'm working her club, making sure all that sweaty-delicious young fuck-energy trickles through the floorboards, now I've got to *babysit* some accidental magus who's metaphysically sliced himself up like some tragic little high school bitch who's got to make her feelings hurt instead of just fuckin' dealing with it." She pulled the compress away. "How's the head?"

Mike touched the welt. Pain shot down the side of his face. "Hurts."

"This'll be worse." She produced a flashlight the size of one of Donnie's cigarillos from her pocket and shone it in his eyes.

"Fuck, cut it out." He pushed her away.

"Need to see if you're concussed. Come on."

The light burned his retinas, but he gritted his teeth until the light snapped off.

"I think you're okay, but I'm also not a doctor."

"What now?"

"Go home, get some actual sleep. Not this bullshit night-sweat nonsense on the couch. Towels? The fuck is wrong with men, I swear. I'll come by around noon, get started."

Mike could barely keep up with the stream of words from her mouth. He just nodded.

"Come on," Evangeline said, grabbing him by the elbow.

Mike's head swam. He tried to stand, wobbled. Would have fallen if not for her, so steady at his side, her grip made of iron.

Maybe he was concussed after all, but he couldn't bring himself to give a shit.

She helped him through the front door. A man sat on the curb, sobbing into a Tandsfield hat, a few black feathers stuck to his body.

"God, Maria," the man cried, then buried his face in his hat.

"Go the fuck home," Evangeline snarled at him. She kicked him in the back. He pitched forward into the gutter, moaning. She rolled her eyes at Mike. "Talk about your messy eaters."

Now he really thought he must be concussed.

She dragged him across the sidewalk and helped him into the back of a dark sedan.

"Thanks, Kara," Mike muttered, then laid across the seat. His eyelids grew heavy. He figured he shouldn't sleep, but couldn't help it. Maybe he'd die and wake up in the world he'd left, where everything made sense and Kara loved him and they were both on the right side of the stars.

Or maybe there'd be nothing. He didn't feel any particular way about it.

The Scavengers

THE SCAVENGERS

MIKE WOKE EARLY with only a lingering headache. Hours until he had to meet Evangeline, if she even showed. If she was real. He checked his phone—no messages—and picked at an unwanted breakfast, thinking he should do something but never settling on what.

The night before was his strangest night yet, but he spent little time obsessing over it. Mostly he was annoyed at Donnie and Keegan for giving him shit, and stamped around until the downstairs neighbor banged on the floor with a broom.

A little after noon, someone knocked. Mike pulled the door open. Evangeline stood there, arms crossed, wearing a black hoodie and leggings, her blonde hair pulled back in a ponytail.

"Hey, jackass," she said, pushing past him. She stopped, sniffing the air. "Huh. So depression has a smell."

"Come on in," Mike muttered.

Evangeline circled the room, turning up her nose at the crumpled towels at the foot of the couch, raising an eyebrow at the bloody wine bottle on the table, picking up a candle and tossing it from hand to hand. Peering at the pale rectangle on the wall where Kara's Condaire print used to be.

"Wound's pretty raw, huh?"

"I guess."

"Got anything to drink in this place?"

Mike checked the fridge—nothing besides a dodgy carton of milk. Once again, he was reminded of how fast his life had fallen apart. He opened the cupboard above the sink, shifted through a few dusty bottles before he found some Josiah.

"Rocks?" Mike called into the living room.

Evangeline was lightly perched on a couch arm, like sitting down was too much of a commitment. "Neat."

Mike poured an ample serving and took it into the living room. Evangeline set it on the coffee table.

"So, what now?" Mike asked. "I admit, I'm at a bit of a loss."

Evangeline scanned the room again, gaze settling on his acoustic. "You play?"

"A little."

Hard to believe she hadn't heard of Modern Love. Then again, maybe she'd stepped out of some off-kilter, parallel world. One where, if he existed at all, he wasn't anyone special.

Not so different, then.

"I can't say no to *her*," Evangeline said, "but that doesn't mean I can't demand additional payment for my services. Play me something."

"Now?"

Evangeline crossed her legs, looking up at him expectantly.

"Okay," Mike said. He grabbed the guitar, plucked a string—still in tune. "This one's called 'Chromaterror.'"

> *Yellow ghosts creep out my closet,*
> *Shaking silver chains,*
> *Green and purple lie in wait*
> *Beyond my windowpane.*
> *I'm shattered by the sunrise,*
> *Laid low by a bouquet,*
> *It's all too much, too much, my darling,*

OUR BLACK HEARTS BEAT AS ONE

*And what I wouldn't give
(Oh, what I wouldn't give)
For a simple touch of grey.*

He met her eyes. She was smiling tightly. Or politely. He couldn't tell, but he was gripped by an urge to bring her in. Please her. Show her that even if it wasn't her choice to help him with whatever the fuck this was, he was worth helping.

Second verse.

*Silent scenes and rainbow screams,
I'm undone by it all.
I'll lock the doors, swallow the key,
Take refuge in these monochrome halls,
But listen please, my darling—*

And here the lyric was *Bree,* and at the last second he knew it was a mistake. Scatting her name was weird enough, but using some diminutive that she maybe hated? But he couldn't stop himself—

—Eve

Evangeline stood abruptly. "Stop."

Mike paused, mid-chord. "I'm sorry."

She took the guitar from him and set it in the corner. "I honestly don't know if that's supposed to be a love song or a breakup song or what, but for fuck's sake, keep my name out of your mouth."

"I know, I thought—"

"You thought you'd endear yourself to me with some pandering bullshit? *Oh, look at the weird little goth girl, I bet nobody with abs has ever sung her a song before!*"

"Um—"

"This is the musical equivalent of giving me a present

you bought for somebody else. Like cross off the other bitch's name and put—" she made a gagging sound, "—Eve? Fucking *Eve*?"

"I wasn't trying—"

"If you knew me, you'd know I don't belong in any kind of song. But tell you what. After this, if you still want to write me something? Cool, maybe by then you won't sound like a fucking robot. And don't try to make me like you. It's gross."

"I'm not—"

"Hush." Evangeline snatched her bourbon off the coffee table and downed it in one gulp. She pushed the glass into Mike's hands. "I'd say give me another, but if I get too drunk, who knows what the fuck might happen?" She held up a finger. "And by that, I mean nothing good for you, understand?"

"Got it."

"Let's get this shit over with so I can go back to hating myself." She abruptly sat down on the couch, as far from his crumpled towels as she could get. "You got the tape recorder?"

"Somewhere." Mike patted his jeans, then found it in his army jacket draped over a dining room chair that would never be used as anything other than a clothes tree again.

"Everybody's got a lost love, but nobody wants to talk about it. A *love found* is probably the easiest. Who do you know that's in love?"

Mike ran a hand through his hair. "Two people come to mind. But they aren't very happy with me right now."

"Who the fuck is?"

The Polyphony

THE POLYPHONY

"**Y**OU'RE A DICK," Donnie said, standing in Keegan's mom's front door. "You know that, right? A complete dick."

The fact he kept it simple, instead of launching into some florid description of how Mike was a diseased, veiny cock spewing chunky yellow discharge, said it all.

Mike waited on the stoop, trying to avoid the rain sluicing off the overhang. They'd driven out to Northport in Evangeline's car, a dark-blue Hattori that, unlike its owner, had no discernable personality whatsoever. Mike had offered to take her on his motorcycle, but Evangeline said there was no fucking way she was riding bitch, but he could give her gas money. The drive took thirty minutes and sucked for everyone involved. Instead of music, they listened to talk radio, the monotone public radio host droning on about some controversy involving the old Bilcher car seat factory. A plan to put up condos. Evangeline didn't seem particularly interested and when she ignored his request to throw on ZBLD, he figured she was punishing them both.

"I was out of line, that shit I said—"

"I know you've been through hell these last couple days, but to dismiss me like that? And Keegan? Who doesn't want to *talk* to you, by the way," he shouted over his shoulder.

"Can you yell at your friend in the garage?" Keegan's mom called back. "The neighbors are going to hear."

"Sorry, Mrs. S," Donnie said, turning back to Mike. "Keegan and I have put just as much into this band as you have, and you know it." Donnie squinted over Mike's shoulder. "Hey, where's your bike?"

Mike'd had Evangeline drop him around the corner, not wanting to explain who she was.

"You're right," Mike said. "I acted like an asshole. I never should've said that shit. I'm sorry."

"And seriously, what was up with you last night? You sounded dead."

"Why I'm here," Mike said. "Can you get Keegan and meet me in the garage?"

"He doesn't want to talk to you."

"Please."

Donnie shook his head, then shut the door.

Mike went around to the detached garage where they usually practiced and let himself in. The inside smelled like mildew and engine oil. He sat in a plastic chair next to the drum kit. Let his eyes wander over all the show fliers taped to the walls. Keegan was obsessive, saved one from every show they'd ever played—except an early gig at the Reformed Consequentialist Church on 67th with Neon Wager, where their flautist interrupted the Modern Love set by running naked across the stage and cannonballing into Keegan's drum kit.

Nobody liked talking about that one.

Still. Hundreds of shows. Two well-received records put out by the indie label Snakes in My Pants. Radio play. They'd built something.

Maybe someday all of this would matter to him again.

Donnie pushed open the door, followed by Keegan, wearing a Gaping Wounds shirt—one of those fucked up math rock bands Mike never really got.

Donnie plopped down on an amp. "Say it to him."

"Sorry about last night," Mike said. "I didn't mean it. I'm just fucked up. That's no excuse, but—"

Keegan held up a hand. "It's fine. I just want to get back to playing." He settled in between Donnie's legs, pulling up his knees to his chest.

"Just like that? After what he said?" Donnie said.

"It was a shitty thing to say," Keegan said. "But it's also shitty to hold it over his head forever."

"I guess." Donnie ran his hands through Keegan's hair. "So, what's up? Feels like you want to talk about more than just last night. And your dickishness."

"Easy," Keegan said.

Mike nodded slowly. "It's sort of about last night. But it's more—shit, I don't know how to say this."

"Take your time," Keegan said. He took off his glasses and cleaned them on the hem of his Gaping Wounds shirt.

Mike took the tape recorder from his pocket, worrying at it with both hands. "Short version is, I did something. After Kara left. I'm trying to figure out how to take it back. 'Cause if I don't, I won't ever be okay, I'll just be this, this—" his body spasmed, something that might've been a sob if he still possessed a heart.

Donnie and Keegan shared a long look.

"Breakups are tough," Donnie finally said. "They're, uh, tough."

"You'll be okay," Keegan added. "Even if it feels like you won't."

"When I broke up with Ashley—"

"Ashley, really?" Keegan said.

"It's relevant, okay? Mike's going through some shit, and that story's—"

"That's what I need," Mike said.

Keegan and Donnie both said, "What?"

Mike held up the recorder. "None of this is going to make any sense, so I'm just going to ask. I need you to tell me the story of how you fell in love."

Keegan frowned. "Mike . . . you were there."

"I know, I—"

"And what, you're gonna put this on the conduit or something?" Donnie said. "No fuckin' way."

"It's not like that—"

The garage door opened. Evangeline poked her head in. "Oh my god, is this where Modern Love practices? Like, squee!"

"Wow," Donnie said. "Whatever's wrong, maybe try working it out between her thighs and leave us alone?"

"I'll tell it," Keegan said, tapping his forehead. "Eidetic memory and all."

"Never waste an opportunity to bring that up," Donnie said.

Mike double-checked the tape recorder. "You ready?"

"Yeah."

He hit *Record.*

"Three years ago," Keegan said. "This was right after the first time we played the Beacon."

Mike shot a glance at Evangeline—she was sitting with her legs crisscrossed underneath her, rapt with attention, presumably because somebody who wasn't Mike was talking.

"Donnie had an extra ticket to Martyrcycle. Originally belonged to *she who shall not be named*, but . . . you don't need that part, do you?"

Mike shook his head. He needed lost love, too, but Donnie and Ashley weren't so much in love as they were addicted to ripping old wounds open then fucking in the blood.

"Donnie asked me to go. I didn't even think it was a date."

"I did," Donnie chimed in. "First time I saw you play a blast beat, I was into it. Although I *did* think you were straight."

Keegan rolled his eyes. "Anyway. We go to the show,

and it's incredible. They even played 'Find Me in Your Entrails,' and they never play that live. We were both amped up—"

"And a little drunk," Donnie added.

"—so we went down to that diner on 4th. Pierson's. And we're recapping the set list, and I realize he's still talking, but I haven't been listening."

"And *I* see this weirdo staring at me, like right through me, so I turn around because I think somebody's getting into a fight at the bar, and then I turn back and he's like *sorry,* and the way he said it was kind of sad, like I wasn't even talking about anything, but he goes *I always want to listen to you.*"

Evangeline uncrossed her legs. "That's sweet."

"Right?" Donnie said. "I thought so. Who the fuck listens to the bassist? I fell in love on the spot."

"Me too."

Mike looked from one friend to another. "Wait, that's it?"

"What do you mean? You've heard this story before."

Evangeline hit STOP on the tape recorder and got up, stretching like a cat. She stifled a yawn. "Well, that'll do it."

"You sure?"

She shot him a withering look.

Mike got up to leave. Donnie and Keegan followed him to the door.

"I'm still pissed at you," Donnie said. "Only *kind of,* though."

"Guess I deserve that. Be seeing you."

Mike and Evangeline got back in her Hattori. "One down," Mike said, reaching for the radio.

She smacked his hand away, then started the car.

"What's next?" Mike said.

"My place." Evangeline glared at him. "Don't get any ideas."

Mike held up his hands. "Don't worry. I don't have any."

Surprisingly, Evangeline didn't live in a crumbling mausoleum but an upscale apartment on the sixth story of a building near the Beacon. They took the elevator. Watching the floors light up was a novelty for Mike, having spent the last few years in a walk-up.

Evangeline put the key in her lock and shot him a look. "Don't touch anything."

"Can I sit down?"

"So demanding." She opened the door.

Unlike the modernist exterior, all glass and strategically placed greenery, her living room screamed *gothic luxe*. Simple, black-painted walls, tantagram carpet. Black candles in silver sconces hung on the walls.

She didn't have a TV.

"Stand there," Evangeline said, pointing to the middle of the room.

Mike went to his designated place. He didn't bother asking if he could hang up his coat. "So what now?"

"Hush." She busied herself lighting candles, pulling drapes. Unfurled a tantagram-covered cloth—just like the one Kara laid in her windowsill at Diamet, a celeman, she'd called it—over the coffee table. She took a stack of cards from a curio cabinet and set them on the cloth. Her lips moved silently, then she motioned for Mike to sit on the floor across from her.

He lowered himself, crossing his legs. Becoming small, childlike. The entire experience seemed slightly humiliating, but he didn't want to risk Evangeline's ire.

"Ever had a tarokki reading before?" Evangeline asked.

"No." Kara asked once, on an early date, and never again when she saw the look on his face.

Evangeline shuffled the cards without looking. "Most people want their fortune read. *Does he like me? Should I break up with him?* That kind of tarokki, it's for people who already know the answer and want to put a metaphysical sheen on their own decisions. *Sorry Chad, it's not me, it's faaate.* This is not that kind of reading. There's more . . . arcane applications."

Mike swallowed. "Like what?"

"This is a variation on a finding spell. I won't bore you with the details. It'd take hours to explain the Nonagromic assertions underpinning the Tarokkic decaschema, but there's someone out there you're supposed to meet. I'm going to conjure the future where you get your heart back, then work backwards from there. Make sense?"

"Yes?"

"Liar. But you're a good sport." She narrowed her eyes. "I should tell you. This isn't cold reading. Things can get intense. You good with that?"

Things were already intense. "Okay."

"Okay?"

"I'm good."

"You say that now." She fluttered the cards from one hand to the other, the sound like a flock of birds taking flight.

The candles guttered, as if from a breeze. The temperature in the apartment dropped.

Mike pulled his army jacket tight. "Uh—"

"Quiet."

Evangeline muttered in a language he didn't recognize, then spread six cards facedown. She closed her eyes, ran circles over her heart, three times one way, thrice in the opposite direction. Then she flipped the cards over, one by one.

When she turned the last card over, she started, letting out a slight yelp.

"What?"

Evangeline drew a long breath. "Nothing." She passed her hand over the cards quickly, then shuffled and repeated the ritual in full.

She flipped the last card again. Grimaced.

Same furtive sweeping motion. Same repetition of the ritual. From her reaction to the way the last card fell?

Same result.

"What the fuck." Evangeline pounded the coffee table. The cards didn't move.

"Seriously, what is it? Something bad? Do I die?"

"You really think I'd be pissed about that?"

Mike eyed her for a long moment. "Whatever your deal is, you don't have to take it out on me. I'm not the one who asked you to help."

Evangeline jumped up and left the room. An unseen door slammed.

Hard.

"Shit." Mike got up, paced the room. The front door called to him. Maybe what he really needed was to go see a shrink. He put a hand to his chest, felt his heartbeat. That was real. He was just fucking traumatized from what Kara did, inventing bizarre shit, maybe stumbling into people who were crazier than him.

But he wasn't hurting anymore. And some of his crazy was shit nobody else would play along with. Yet Evangeline was.

The walls groaned—water running. Then stopped. A door opened and Evangeline came out, head down, hair shrouding her face. She dabbed at an eye with a tissue.

"Hey, I'm—"

"You were right. You're not the person I should be mad at."

"Thanks."

"But I'm still mad, okay?" She sat on the sofa, reached for the cards.

"Wait," Mike said. "What was that last card? I want to know."

"Doesn't matter. It's not about you."

"You said it's my future." He gestured at the cards. "How is it not?"

"Because it's about *me,* okay? And I don't want to fucking talk about it. Sit."

About her? So she was in his future, somehow. Mike wasn't as pissed as she was about it, but he wasn't exactly enchanted by the idea, either.

He put it out of his mind. "Let's keep going."

Evangeline bowed her head and clasped both hands together. She whispered more strange words, quick and guttural, then picked up the six cards on the table, collapsing them into a single stack.

"This is where things get real. Just remember, visions can't hurt you."

"Okay?"

"You're going to pick a card. You'll—see things. Hear things. Just try not to piss yourself on my carpet."

"I'm not going to piss—"

"Good, because if you do, you'll be cursed." She cast him a serious glance. "Not joking. That rug is, uh, *special.* And easily offended."

Mike wondered if he should really be sitting on it.

Evangeline held out the cards. "Close your eyes. Picture your heart beating in your chest. And choose."

Mike shut his eyes. The goreslick pig's heart loomed large in his mind's eye.

Pulsing.

His hand brushed over the sleek surface of the cards and pulled one from the stack.

A thunderclap resounded between his ears, and he fell headlong into darkness. Screaming wind rushed by, like he was hurtling impossibly fast. Through nothing and into nothing.

He didn't piss himself.

Everything slowed down. The darkness melted. A plain desert landscape, untroubled by plant life, stretched away in either direction. Six moons shone down from a violet slash of sky.

He wasn't sure what to do, so he walked. His head was spinning from the fall. He passed a bundle of bones and rags clawing the sand without flesh or pulse or obvious means of animation. A shadow drifted over the landscape, insubstantial yet intimating the silhouette of four men in a line, hands fused together. The shadow swirled about, voices gibbering in the wind, then blew away. He passed Donnie and Keegan, waxen like figures out of Panclock's Peculiarities. Donnie was passing back and forth through a door frame that led nowhere, Keegan burying his head in the sand.

Part of Mike wanted to go to them, but these were not his friends, just automatons, acting out some lonely play, its meaning too obscure to parse.

He rubbed his fingers together, felt something between. He held up the card to the moonlight. It bore the image of a man dressed in rags, riding a fine, white horse, and holding a sword high.

The Tattered Knight, it said.

Hoofbeats exploded across the desert floor. Mike turned just in time to see a rider bearing down on him, kicking up sand, raising a sword.

It bit into his neck.

Then the desert fell away, back into that strange rushing darkness, hurtling faster and faster and—

"Mike," Evangeline said softly.

He opened his eyes. Flat on his back, staring up at the ceiling. She was bent over him.

Stroking his cheek.

She must've realized he was conscious because she paused, glancing at her hand with disgust.

"How long was I out?" Mike managed.

She helped him sit up, gave him a glass of water. "Three hours. I've never seen anything like that."

"Three hours," Mike repeated, rubbing his temples. A stray Tarokki card lay next to him. He flipped it over—*The*

Tattered Knight, same as in his vision. "So what does this mean?"

Evangeline took the card from him and set it on top of the deck, then put the whole affair back in her curio cabinet. "Your next story."

"I don't get it, how does this help?"

Evangeline gave him her phone. "I took a picture. Don't worry, I can read High Terrine."

Mike looked down at the phone—him, shirtless, a cluster of eldritch symbols carved into his chest. The wounds were deep, to the bone, weeping blood. Like he was looking inside himself.

His hand shook. Evangeline snatched the phone away before he could drop it.

"Here," she said, pulling him up and helping him into the hallway. They walked a few feet before she turned on a light.

He was looking into a mirror, Evangeline practically holding him up. His skin was pale, hair plastered to his forehead.

She gently took the hem of his shirt and pulled it up. Light scars covered his body, but the wounds had mostly healed. In three hours. He leaned heavily against the wall.

"How?"

"Magic." She helped him back to the living room, letting him sit on the couch this time. "I'm going to get you a big fucking glass of Josiah, then I'll track down the guy you need to meet. Just sit here and try not to think too much."

She breezed out of the room, happier than he'd ever seen her. Mike couldn't help but think the sight of him bleeding from a dozen wounds had enhanced her mood.

"He killed me," he called to her. "In the vision."

Evangeline poked her head back in. "So?"

"Is this guy going to murder me?"

"Don't worry," she said, smiling. "I've never been that lucky."

The Tattered
Knight

THE TATTERED KNIGHT

THE BURLY, HEAVY-BROWED man at the coffee shop table was wearing Mike's jacket. A twin, but for the dark stains and fraying cuffs. He didn't look up when they entered, instead peering down into a porcelain cup that looked like a child's toy before him, fingers tapping an unheard rhythm on its saucer. Shortly, he gave a minute wave, confirming he was the man they were there to meet, and not some ape escaped from a laboratory experiment where they dressed him in weathered clothes and taught him a man's manners.

He seemed more than capable of carrying out the Tarokki-born vision of Mike's end.

"You want anything?" Mike asked Evangeline, nodding at the barista behind the counter.

"Just his story."

The drive from Benoit had been long—over six hours. Mike tried to make conversation, but she ignored him. Bored, he looked at the billboards—mostly blank. Benoit and the ancillary towns around it were currently crumbling into iron-flecked dust. The fact they'd even found a place to meet the man had been a minor miracle, though the coffee shop looked little like the one Mike had worked in once upon a time—no hand-written blackboards, pastry-filled glass cases. This shop was simple, spare.

But the coffee smelled good. Mike got himself a cup, Evangeline offering a smile to the cashier when she assured the woman she didn't need anything, then approached the table.

"If he asks, you're a journalist," Evangeline whispered.

"What—"

"Argo Gabrogian?" Evangeline asked, pulling out a chair.

The man looked up—beetle brows, stubbly jaw, a thick head of wirebrush hair streaked with grey, and a thin, straight nose that seemed out of place and vaguely resembled an ancient Terrine sculpture. A scar slashed down his cheek, forming a jagged white canyon where no hair grew. His eyes were deep-set and unreadable, lending his visage the aspect of a funeral mask. He smelled faintly of ashes and earth.

"I am he," the man muttered. He had a thick Mruatian accent.

Nobody said anything about the matching jackets.

"We spoke on the phone," Evangeline said. "We didn't talk payment, I—"

"No payment. I've tried for years to get the media to listen, to tell people what their world is really like. They would rather ignore."

"Fair enough." Mike put the recorder on the table. "Just get to it, then?"

Gabrogian grunted.

Mike hit Record.

The man rubbed his temples.

And began.

The thing you must understand about Benoit is, it's always been falling down from the moment the first settlers arrived in their wagons after long months fighting the elements, disease. When they came upon the Steelhead, it was late summer. The river teemed with fish. They stripped and washed themselves. Built great

cookfires, sending the smoke of a hundred salmon up into the sky like an offering to the gods.

Maybe it was. And maybe it wasn't enough. In their merriment, they hadn't noticed the clouds rolling in. Heavy clouds, pregnant with rain and electricity. That night, lying in their bedrolls around the fire, free from the cursed cramped confines of the wagons, they felt the first drops and thought little of it.

Then the deluge began in earnest. Sheets of rain fell from the sky, swamping their camp. The wind howled, rising in anger like a god denied, beating at the shutters of the wagons, rocking them back and forth. The winds swirled faster and faster, becoming something more.

And worse.

The tornado killed half their number outright. One man was impaled by a broken spoke and lingered for days, but in the end the storm claimed him too, long after its dwindling. In the morning, the survivors took stock. Little left, their mighty wagons broken down to timber and metal shavings.

Because they had no means of leaving, they stayed.

That is what I mean, when I say Benoit has always been falling down. The first Benoit, the city formed when a wagon train circled on the banks of the Steelhead, lasted less than a day. A new Benoit raised up, and another, and another—fires, floods, and more tornadoes wiped the slate clean. Over and over again, Benoit saw a succession of new cities built atop the corpses of the last. The city surrounding us is just one Benoit, amid yet another destruction, this time by forces more relentless than the tornado that fell upon that wagon train.

Economics.

From the start, Benoit's bent was to destruction and decay. Maybe the city's nature awoke something buried here, awaiting its moment. Or maybe the city's nature birthed it. I do not know how such things come to be.

Only that it is my sole and sworn purpose on this earth to end them.

For years, I've traveled from city to city, engaged in curious transactions. Not for money, although that's always a requirement. No, simply because there are things in this world whose existence I cannot countenance. Things that hide in the dark and forlorn places, making a mockery of reason. The world should not contain such things, so I cut them out.

This is how I first came to Benoit.

Once there was a man named Moston. A plain and uninteresting man, who should've led a plain and uninteresting life. The only thing of him that mattered was his love for a woman named Annelina. What she saw in him, I do not know, but his love was returned fiercely. I knew the man little, but of this I have no doubt.

Only love could drive a man to such foolishness.

One day, something from the dark and forlorn places found Annelina. She disappeared. Moston was inconsolable. The police did what they could—nothing— because the source of her disappearance was readily apparent.

They called it Volscher. You may have heard the name, urban legends being one of Benoit's few contemporary exports.

Back then, people would scarcely speak the name, but everyone knew what it meant. Certain places were claimed as his. He had a sigil, a bisected figure eight. If this sigil appeared carved into a steel beam or a chunk of concrete, the citizenry avoided the area with the sort of devoted assiduousness that would be the envy of the most orthodox Prostrato. Such places were always disused, forgotten—empty factories, burned-out houses. Acceptable losses, though they proliferated with time. Everyone lived with it quietly, and no one thought they might do anything about it.

OUR BLACK HEARTS BEAT AS ONE

Until Moston, and his broken heart.

He found me through business contacts and made a proposition. I was skeptical, but agreed. This smelled like superstition. I doubted the existence of this Volscher, and if it did exist, I did not believe it wielded the power Moston thought. I'd encountered many things that should not be, with the sharpest teeth and claws. Hundreds of them I'd faced down, in their sanctums deep beneath the earth. They'd touched me, slightly, but nothing more than that. I say this not as braggadocio, but simple fact: nothing of earth or sky can kill me but time.

I never expected Volscher might do worse.

Moston told me of a supposedly claimed place, a broken trestle along the Steelhead at the end of Elscolm Avenue. I took his money and left him in his rowhouse to mourn. That place—dreary, filled with dead flowers, the furniture covered with yellowing sheets. Vengeance would not be the salve he sought. Nothing could help him.

At the trestle, I found Volscher's sigil scored into the wood. And profaned it with a swipe of my knife. I stood there in the wind, listening to traffic cross the New Bridge, less than a mile away, waiting for him to come—whether from the clouds or the earth or the depths of the river, I did not know.

The first sign of something wrong was the wind—it did not stop blowing, but I stopped feeling it.

Strange.

Next, all the colors of the world retreated. The moon, once fat and full, paled until it resembled a circle of gauze hung in a paper sky. The water turned to vapor. Though I could still see the fading lights of cars crossing the New Bridge, no longer could I hear their horns and motors.

I ran. Down the trestle, though my boots made no sound. By the time I reached the end, mere feet, the world was gone. Darkness surrounded me.

Now, *I thought.* Now he must come.

But he did not.

I heard nothing. Saw nothing. Felt nothing.

Too late, I learned this Volscher was not kith and kin to the many fanged and clawed things I'd slain. Not something that offended and infringed upon my conception of what the world must be, but something entirely beyond it. Was that where I was now? Transported—no, snipped out—and left far beyond the borders of where our reality eventually ends?

I know not how long I lingered there, in that nowhere. I neither slept, nor ate, nor missed either. With no external enemy to battle, I faced things within myself, in the dark and forlorn places within my mind. See these marks on my forearm? Battle scars, but not the kind you might think. I made them myself, with my own knife. Yes, this one. See how sharp it is? I sank this very steel into my arm, deep. I bled. In that cursed nowhere, I bled.

The sight made me angry.

I tore my shirt into makeshift tourniquets. The bleeding slowed. Perhaps I'd not cut as deep as I thought. Maybe something within me stayed my hand. Better angels, you could call it. Or not—such things don't need names.

Knowing now I had an escape, if I chose, I closed my eyes—little difference it made—and focused on my anger, at what I'd been driven to, at how he'd taken me from the world I was sworn to set right, to remake how any benevolent god would've. I clutched the knife tightly.

Then I began to cut.

See the blade? See how sharp it is? This steel could cut through anything.

Why couldn't it cut through nothing?

I wasn't lost in some infinite void, but in the belly of a beast made from the opposite of everything there is. I slashed, and sliced, and poured every last dollop of anger within me into every swipe of the knife. My will, my intention, realized. Corporealized.

OUR BLACK HEARTS BEAT AS ONE

No matter how the world twists and contorts itself, I shall do what I wilt.

After a time, something far off began to whimper.

Then to howl.

The howling grew to a great keening yowl, louder than a wounded beast, a battlefield, a nation crying out in pain for the injustices done under the fog of war. Louder than anything imaginable, a universe *entire being torn down to atoms, then torn apart again, until all its constituent parts could no longer cleave each to the other. The clamor grew and grew, filling the nothing until it was no longer nothing at all, because it was filled with pain, and pain is the stuff of our universe, the most fundamental building block of existence.*

I wasn't killing it. I was making it exist.

Soon, the noise faded. A breeze buffeted my cheeks. I opened my eyes and found myself standing on the trestle, daytime now, the sun shimmering off the surface of the Steelhead. I looked for the symbol I'd profaned, that bisected figure eight, but it was gone—not even a sign of its obliteration remained.

I'd changed, however. My hair touched my shoulders, my beard grew to my chest. Fingernails twisted into claws, like so many of the things I've killed. I wandered down Elscolm Avenue until I found a newspaper box and checked the date.

Three years, I'd been gone.

I came here. I had no money and looked every bit the vagrant time had made me. Shella took pity on me. Here I sat, had my first cup of coffee in years. A biscuit. And then, it may surprise you, but I lay my head on this very table and cried until my body shook.

After composing myself, I went to find Moston, to tell him I'd finally put paid to Volscher, but he was not in his rowhouse. No one was, nor had been, in a very long time. The windows were shattered, the once dustcovered-

furniture smashed to bits. All the houses on his old block were the same. I did not ask anyone where he went—the truth of it was plain.

After I disappeared, he took it upon himself to avenge his lost love. Even though, if I failed, what could he hope to do? And yet, he tried. I'm sure of it. His love for her was the only part of him. There was nothing else.

Whatever he did, whenever he did it, Moston succumbed to the same nothingness that took me for a time. Perhaps he found his Annelina there. Maybe they were flung back into this world when I was and left ever-crumbling Benoit behind for good.

Or maybe they still linger there, forever lost in the dead belly of the Anti-Thing.

All I know is I held up my end of the contract. Moston's love was avenged.

Mike hit *Stop*. "That's a story, all right."

Gabrogian fixed his gaze on some far-off point. "I supposed I'll see it in the papers."

Mike shot Evangeline a look, but she was worrying at her nails. "Sure." He pushed his chair back. "I, uh—it's a long drive back."

Evangeline put a hand on Gabrogian's bulky forearm. "Thank you."

"You have my number," Gabrogian said. "If you ever need . . . services."

Mike flashed back to the tunnel. The Rat King. *Things that should not be.* "I'll keep that in mind." He headed for the door.

"Wait," Gabrogian said.

Mike shot a wary look over his shoulder, half-expecting a bullet from the man a Tarokki deck said would kill him. "Yeah?"

"A coda, of sorts. If you'd hear it."

Mike came back to the table. "Sure. Should I turn the recorder back on?"

"No. Call this trivia." Gabrogian sipped coffee, long gone cold. "As you see, I have not left Benoit. This Volscher was like nothing I've encountered before. So, it is imperative I understand it."

Mike leaned on the chairback, wondering if any of this could be understood by anyone.

"I've spent years—longer than I was gone—researching Benoit's history. I can tell you where the cobblestones in the Livery district were quarried. Who sat in the mayor's office, going back two hundred years. Even the architect who designed the old bridge, of which remains not but a rusting trestle. No one knows more about this city than me, but I cannot tell you from whence this Volscher came, or what it was.

"But what I can say is this. You recall my story of the first Benoit? The man impaled upon a broken spoke, lingering for days, feverish and septic, green and gangrenous?"

"Yes," Mike and Evangeline said at once.

"I learned a little of that man. He was an Allemander, little more than a year upon the continent that would claim his life. A cobbler by trade. His family name?"

"What?"

"Volscher."

The word hung in the still air of the coffee shop.

"Now," Gabrogian said quickly, "I don't think the entity I encountered was this man, transmuted by death into a new and strange form. I've seen all that death can do. But maybe this creature was the ghost of what happened to him. Maybe his rot became something unto itself." Gabrogian laughed quietly. "Us fools, with our science and reason. We can describe the processes that make the earth turn on its axis, the waves ebb and flow. A plane fly, a furnace flare. But do we understand them?"

"Someone told me once," Evangeline said, "science is the what. You must look elsewhere for the why."

"Or nowhere. *Why* is a false god." Gabrogian stood, put a hand out.

Mike took it. Gabrogian's grip was firm, but not crushing—a man who had no need to prove what he was.

"I hope you find what you're looking for," Gabrogian said.

"You as well."

"Come on," Evangeline said, pulling his sleeve.

Mike gave Gabrogian one last look, then made for the door. They went down the block and got in Evangeline's car. It was already getting dark.

He chewed over the fantastical story. Bizarre, meandering. Improbable in the extreme.

Any less probable than four men fused together? A mystic behind a bank of box fans? Cutting out his own heart but still thinking, breathing, semi-living?

Less probable than Kara leaving him in the first place?

"Can't wait for another six hours of scintillating conversation," Evangeline said, spinning the car around. They drove back by the café. Mike half-expected it to be empty, boarded-up, a bisected figure eight spray-painted across the plywood.

But no—Gabrogian, seated at the same table, the coffee cup pushed away.

Head in his hands.

Mike dreamed he was lost and wandering in nothingness, but he was not alone, for across that amaranthine stretch of nothing an unending multitude of men and women crawled about on hands and knees, calling softly as to a skittish dog who'd only run when chased, and intermittently they'd sit up and cry out to the anti-heavens and beat their chests, but their hands became lost in the great gaping cavities left as memorials to the extractions of their organs, and none could call out their grief with a breastbone drumbeat but their cries grew louder and louder as their lungs expanded into the chest-space where once hearts pumped and pulsated and became overworked not by the demands of the body but those of the mind, that psychic tonnage applied not to the liver nor the kidneys nor—

"Hey," Evangeline said.

Mike yawned, rubbed sleep from his eyes. They were on the highway, a long straight-away through barren flatlands, mountains looming to their right. "Hey."

"You passed out for a while. But I'm bored and there's nothing on the radio."

"You want me to entertain you?"

Evangeline smirked. "Distract me, at least."

"Okay." He sat there, numb and dumb. "That guy was terrifying. This thing still work if the story's bullshit?"

"You didn't believe him?"

"Not what I mean. He clearly believes his own story, which makes the whole thing even scarier."

"And you don't? With everything you've seen so far?

"I don't know." Mike scratched the back of his neck. "I mean, I've heard the story before, but it's an urban legend. It'd be like, like me telling somebody about the Darlingham Monkey-Man, but then I beat him to death and dragged his corpse home and made jerky. That's two leaps of logic."

"That the thing exists, and you're a badass?"

"Right."

She was quiet a long moment. "Can you really see a guy like that bragging about something that didn't happen?"

Mike's turn to be quiet. Then—

"I guess you're right." The idea was mind-numbing. Or boggling. He felt like he'd just slipped right out of the world he knew into a parallel one, where nothing made sense.

Like that old Chatty Cathys song—*this isn't my bedroom, this isn't my bed, this isn't my head . . .*

"You're not talking," Evangeline said. "That was the deal. You talk, I drive." She waggled the steering wheel, sending the car yawing across the double-yellow line and back again.

"Watch it!"

"What? You can do a shitty job on your thing, but I can't do a shitty job on mine?"

"You're crazy." He shifted in his seat. "What do you want to talk about?"

Evangeline considered this a moment. "Tell me about her. Kara."

"Why?"

"It's another two hours to the city. And since I'm doing you these favors, I'd like to know why. Everybody's had their heart broken. Why is she so special you felt the need to do all this?" Evangeline gestured vaguely at nothing.

Mike flipped the visor, tamped down rumpled strands of hair. "Because I loved her."

"Not good enough."

And it wasn't. Mike had been in love before, surely. Nothing approaching the feelings he'd had for Kara, like he'd unlocked some new and heretofore-unknown capability inside himself. A depth of love he couldn't have imagined. How could he explain that?

Evangeline took both hands off the wheel, driving with her knees. Fished a chapstick from her purse and applied it to her lips.

"Tell me something. Just something about her."

"Right," Mike muttered, staring out through the windshield at the long, flat distance in front of them. Then—

"Here's something."

"Yeah?"

"She was there when everything started happening for

me. We were playing these basement shows, splitting our cut of the door with three other bands, and then ZBLD got hold of our demo and started playing it. One minute she was our whole audience in some shit bar, the next we were getting interviewed on the radio and playing the big clubs. She knew me when I was Mike Mallory, not *Mike Mallory*."

"So you only look at her in the context of your own life."

"Fuck off. It's more like, she loved me when I was nobody and loved me when I was somebody and I can't figure out how the fuck I changed into someone she couldn't love anymore. See," he twisted around in his seat to look at her, "I'm not thinking about Kara in the *context of my life*. I'm thinking about *me* in the context of *hers*. That's what I can't get my head around." He pounded his fist on the dash. "How did I fuck up so badly?"

Days ago, tears would've come easily. But now?

Mike couldn't find anything approaching a feeling in his chest and it made him want to push the door open, dive out onto the pavement, let the asphalt twist and tear him into something that wasn't alive anymore.

Beset by nothingness, Gabrogian turned the knife on himself first, didn't he?

"What if she told you?" Evangeline said quietly. "You get back, she's waiting at the apartment, not to reconcile, but to give you the explanation you think you're owed?"

"I should be so lucky."

"And what if it doesn't satisfy you?"

"Huh?"

"Think about it. What could she possibly tell you that would make everything all right?"

Mike stared out at the never-ending landscape. "Nothing."

"The fundamental problem with relationships," Evangeline said, "is understanding. People, and I'm talking about me here, can't even understand ourselves. Or the world itself—you heard Gabrogian. He's running around in sewers slitting throats because he can't understand anything. And to understand another person? To even conceptualize them as something entirely outside ourselves?

"How is that even possible?"

Mike hung his head. How, indeed. Maybe people thought they understood, but how many lies does one tell just to force ourselves out of bed every day?

Maybe that was the most fucked up thing. The thing he couldn't countenance. Knowing he'd never known Kara at all. He'd loved her, kissed her and held her, but no matter how he put himself inside her, he couldn't see what was in there.

A fool to try.

Maybe he was better off like this. Star-bound to live a loveless life, like every other human being on the planet, except his curse was to *know* this, to see behind the curtain, to know magic animated nothing. Just pistons and gears, a traveling chemical show upon which we all impressed meaning out of terror and boredom.

The greatest fool of all is he who cannot fool himself, and woe, woe to that sad shell, that husk.

"I wasn't going to do this," Evangeline said.

And wrenched the wheel hard to the right.

They sat on the hood of her car, a few yards off the highway down an access road, the mountains ahead purpling in the setting sun.

They came plain as penitents, no booze, no smokes, nothing but themselves, the burning catalyst of life itself fleeing their gaze. Man and woman, clothed yet more naked than any had ever been. Behind them, dust curled up into the sky, the echo of their sudden detour into the gravel. A bird bisected the otherwise empty sky, let out a cry, and then spun like a turbine to earth in search of sustenance.

Evangeline turned to him. Something inside Mike shivered, a phantom hint of feeling. She opened his jacket and took the recorder from the inside pocket, setting it on the hood between them.

"I can't fucking believe I'm doing this," Evangeline said.

"Doing what?"

"Your last story. A love lost? I've got that. Why do you think I was there in the first place? Some things, they're not survivable. You can either kill yourself or kill what you've been, but you can't keep on. Not like that.

"I never thought I'd talk about this. But," she gestured at the mountains, "it feels right. If I've been a bitch to you, it's because I'm so much worse to myself. Me, now? It's the best I can do. And maybe it's totally fucking insane, but I might be able to do better, if I just tell somebody, anybody, even goddamn you what happened.

"So."

"Hey." Mike went to pat her back and then thought better of it. "I appreciate you helping me with this, and I know what a big deal it must be for you."

"Ugh, this is some *Eve* shit again. Just shut the fuck up and listen."

She clicked *Record*.

The Mirrors

THE MIRRORS

"THIS IS IT. *Your story of loss. I've kept it close. But it doesn't serve me anymore, and if it serves you?*

Maybe some good can come out of it.

I can't tell you how I lost Raphael without telling you why I loved him in the first place. Otherwise, this wouldn't be a proper story, just a progression of facts: we met on this date. Went to this restaurant. Went to another. Wandered through Dulcette Park. Celebrated an anniversary. Moved in. Fought and made up. Drank wine on the rooftop. Breakfast. Massages. Lied and said we were happy. Girls night. Wine. I'm sleeping on the couch. Long talks. Lie more.

And then on this *date—*

See? That's a timeline. Not a story.

Back then, I was in real estate, mostly because I'd no real idea what I wanted to do. Art interested me, in a passing way. Went to a gallery opening one night, just to play the sophisticate. A pretty boy with a scarf around his neck led me between paintings. All abstract, nothing to hold on to, and though my date wrung every drop of meaning out of those simple swatches of primary color, I was bored to tears.

Still drank enough to go home with that pompous, beautiful boy with the scarf circled around his neck.

I woke up before him. Snuck out, holding my heels, softly shutting the door behind me.

87

And that's when I met Raphael; exiting his own apartment across the hall, decked out in neon green jogging shorts with sweatbands around his wrists. His clothing was ridiculous, but he was tall, lithe, gorgeous black curls falling over his forehead.

He swiped them away to get a better look at me. "Morning," he said—quiet, like he knew exactly what I was up to. "Friend of Trevor's, I take it?"

Oh, so that was his name. He was in my phone as Scarf Boy.

"Sort of," I said, smiling despite myself.

He smiled back and jerked a thumb at the elevator bank. "Can I offer you a lift?"

"I wouldn't want to interrupt your run." He'd turned slightly, showing the backs of his taut calves—no, I would not want to interrupt that.

"Oh, I'm doing the waterfront loop. Can't beat the view." He jingled keys. "Are you on the way, by chance?"

I lived fifteen minutes in the opposite direction, a condo on Granger Hill that I shared with two other girls. "Sort of?"

"Good enough."

We took the elevator to the parking garage. Raphael drove a brand-new Voigt Ivory. Silver, with a rag top. I didn't know much about cars, but the way it shone under the garage lights? I could appreciate its beauty, even if I didn't understand it.

He opened the door for me. Scarf Boy had only opened another bottle of wine and taken up three-quarters of the bed. The interior was beige, leather. It smelled like heaven.

It was cold out, so we drove with the top up. He dropped me off at my building. One of my roommates—Mara, an agreeable girl who worked reception at a dance academy downtown and sustained herself on the empty promise of becoming an instructor someday—was coming out.

"Thanks for the ride," I said.

"My pleasure. Hope this isn't too forward, but you and Trevor?"

"Not serious. Not anything."

"Then we should do this again sometime."

We traded numbers. Raphael peeled away in his fancy silver Voigt.

"Hot date?" Mara asked, suddenly at my elbow.

"Not at first," I said. "But it might've turned into one."

The thing you have to realize is, I met Raphael in the most embarrassing circumstances possible. Maybe that situation wouldn't bother you, but you're a guy. It's different. Getting caught ditching out on a perfectly adequate hookup? And his neighbor, no less. I should've been mortified.

But he wasn't. Later on, when we were an actual couple and people asked how we met, he didn't laugh and compliment himself for saving me from a walk of shame.

He just said, we bumped into each other one morning. Aren't I lucky?

First date, some deconstructed pierogi place, I was nervous about running into Scarf Boy again—dating his neighbor and all—but Raphael kept refilling my glass and telling charming stories about him, his finance job, little facts about the city. I forgot scarves ever existed.

Dessert came—some kind of soufflé. It was delicious. He was delicious. Hell, the air tasted sweet, every breath tinged with the slightest hint of sugar.

I don't mind telling you it was the best fucking date I've ever been on.

He handled the check while I was in the ladies' room, because of course he did, that was Raphael. Holding doors, pulling out chairs. Consummate gentleman.

He stayed the gentleman when he drove me home and kissed me goodnight without trying to come in.

Sweeter than the soufflé.

Mara was up watching some reality show—you know the one where Sadie Satin married that cricket player, Derec something? I sat with her and she asked me three thousand questions about the date.

I woke up the next morning and realized I'd no idea the last time she'd been on one of her own.

Raphael and I kept seeing each other. When we weren't together, I couldn't get him out of my mind. I re-read his texts over and over. Silly, I know, but pretty much all my relationships had been one Scarf Boy or another. I'd get interested in someone, but I wouldn't stay interested.

Raphael wasn't like that. I was all in, all the time.

We were spending lots of nights at my place, and my other roommate—Kenzie, who hardly ever left her room—was getting passive aggressive, like "oh, Raphael's coming over again?" So yeah, it was time we started spending nights at his place, but it made me nervous thinking about running into Scarf Boy.

"You know he moved out, right?" Raphael said, on that first drive over to his place.

"Sorry?"

"Your, uh—" he rubbed his chin, "—friend? From the day we met?"

Fuck yes.

Raphael's apartment was gorgeous. Homey, comfy. Smelled amazing. Something about the space, the way he arranged everything, really flowed. Spare, but he was a devotee of that guru Lissa Tynantz, you know her book, The Lesser Life?

Oh, and?

He was the only man I'd ever met who kept flowers in his house. Seriously. Redagalias in a vase by the door.

OUR BLACK HEARTS BEAT AS ONE

We spent the weekend together, which ended too soon.

*"I can't imagine another moment without you,"
Raphael said, holding me close that last morning, while I
pretended to squirm against his grip, protesting that I
really had to get to work, but I couldn't imagine a moment
without him, either.*

*I went back to work but I never really left that
apartment. Could still feel his arms around me. Could still
feel him inside of me. He was all I thought about.*

*We went everywhere together. Did everything
together. A hot-air balloon ride, even. When I had a bad
day, he showed up with flowers and chocolates and this
wonderful soft look in his eyes without me even asking.
He always knew how to make me smile.*

*These were all the good parts. For weeks, it was
nothing but the good parts.*

*Huh? That's what Kara used to say? Weird. You know
as well as I do it can't just be the good parts. There's got
to be other shit. Shit-shit. Took longer for it to boil to the
surface with Raph, but it did all the same.*

*I organized a happy hour, this super-swanky wine
bar in Bunker Station, so all my friends could meet him.
Mara, a couple coworkers, some other chicks from
college. A dozen girls, all there to meet my dreamy new
boyfriend with six-pack abs who drove a Voigt Ivory.*

*Raphael brought himself, even though I'd told him to
invite all the boys. Begged him, because he had to have
someone we could hook Mara up with. Didn't he?*

*Except 'the Boys' didn't exist. "Friends are just
distractions," he said. And then looked me in the eyes,
hand stroking my cheek. "Besides, you really want
anyone else competing for my time?"*

Competing.

*I should've run for the exits. Or let Tiffany have him,
she was practically in heat, squeezing his arms like we
were in the produce section picking out rainmelons. I*

almost dumped my wine glass all over that bitch's head, but restrained myself. Somehow.

"You really don't have any friends?" I asked again on the drive home.

Raphael turned to meet my eyes. "I've got you," he said, patting my thigh.

Then looked away to the road ahead.

Look, I know that was a red flag. But you have to understand, he was sweet, and when he looked at me, I was like the only thing in the entire fucking universe. The sun, the stars, all of it.

We started talking about moving in together. Raphael threw himself into this new project with his usual zeal. We spent a night on opposite ends of the couch, playing footsie and word association games while he jotted down notes on a yellow legal pad.

"Name three things you can't live without."

"Hmm," I said, ticking them off on my fingers. "Clawfoot bathtub. Granite countertops. And laundry. And you. Oh, that's four."

"That's okay." He leaned in for a kiss. "Four's my lucky number."

We mostly agreed on everything—three bedrooms, two full baths, in case we started a family. A garage, to keep that Voigt in tip-top shape. A big backyard for our imaginary dog to romp around—I'd always loved Stretherford Torchhounds, but they need a lot of room.

At the end of the night, Raph passed me the legal pad—he'd drawn a little picture of our fantasy house. Plus me and him, standing outside with a dog at our feet. He wasn't the greatest artist in the world, but it was so sweet.

"I'm putting this on my refrigerator," I said.

Of course I never thought we'd find exactly what we wanted. The whole point of the exercise was to dream big. But Raphael called the next day, said he'd found a place.

OUR BLACK HEARTS BEAT AS ONE

It was kind of weird, me being in real estate, but I hadn't started looking yet.

He picked me up after work, beaming. We drove out to Chennewick Gardens. I know, suburbia. Traffic was rough because of an overturned semi—"not a regular thing, don't worry," Raphael said. I was watching everything out the window, thinking how it was kind of nice. Not any place I'd ever wanted to live, but I never wanted to date a man I met sneaking out of another one's apartment either, so there you go.

Sometimes the universe gives you things you've never considered, and they're great.

Raphael pulled up to this house, cocked his chin out the window, and damned if it wasn't the exact house he'd drawn.

"What do you think?" Raphael asked.

I kissed him in response.

Things moved quickly after that. I gave notice at the condo. Mara didn't take it well, things got a little tense one night, she actually yelled at me, so I stomped off to get a drink. Ended up at some dive on Garrison. I walked up to the jukebox but this guy's already there, and you know what he plays?

So yeah, I lied. I had heard of you before. Used to have the t-shirt, even.

The jukebox guy turned around, and it's Scarf Boy. I'm wondering how fucking fast I can throw back my beer and disappear into the night, but he just said hi.

"Hey." I've got my beer in my hand, wondering if I should have my keys instead. You know, the sharpest one poked between your knuckles? You're a guy, you've probably never had to do that.

Oh, that's right, the rock and roll thing. Whatever.

"Buy you a drink?" Scarf Boy said.

"It's a free country."

We grabbed stools at the bar. He dragged his a couple inches away. Respectful distance.

He really wasn't that bad of a guy.

Oh, and all this time, you're singing in the background. "Liminal Gods."

Maybe if you'd snuck my name in there instead of "Chromaterror" I wouldn't have gone off on you like that.

Scarf Boy drummed his fingers on the bar. "Things working out with Raph?"

"They're great."

"That's good. That's really good. Umm—"

"Out with it."

Awkwardness like this, I was thinking he was going to profess his love for me.

"Raphael got me kicked out."

My first instinct was to laugh. Raphael? Seriously? If this was some end run to get back in my pants, it's the saddest, most pathetic attempt I've ever seen.

It's not.

Raphael started making noise complaints. A lot. Then Scarf Boy came home one day to a house full of smoke, an overflowing ashtray on his coffee table. The building manager showed up at his door while he was airing the place out, gave him his thirty-day notice.

Day he moved out, Raphael's standing outside his door, watching him lug furniture.

Smiling.

Hearing this, I'm nodding along, but I'm really laughing at this pathetic little boy and his what had happened was *stories. I finished my drink and went home. Mara was already in bed, and when the moving trucks came the next day, she made herself scarce. I left a note saying sorry and moved in with Raphael.*

Things were good. We made our bed for the first time and got sidetracked by a pillow fight that turned into something else. Then got into an actual fight over the living room—I wanted to hang up some art, Raphael wanted to keep things "minimalist." I let him have his way because it didn't matter that much to me. We were finally living together. I tacked the picture he drew of our old future house, now our real house, to the fridge and called it a day.

I was washing dishes when he came in to get a drink. "Hey," I called over my shoulder, twisting around to look at him, really look at him, this magical man of mine.

He was standing in front of the refrigerator, staring at the picture on the door. Eyebrow-raised, like that old actor Ibsen Cress? The dad on Takes One to Know One? *"I got outta bed for this?"*

No, I never really watched it either, but you know what I'm talking about, right?

Next day, the picture was gone. I never saw it again.

Other than that, the first month's great. Second month, too. Raphael'd been driving me to work, but I started taking the train somewhere around month three. Our schedules were different, so it made sense. What I told myself at the time.

Really, I was losing my goddamn mind.

See, we've got this house, and it's perfect. I've got this boyfriend, and he's perfect. Everything's perfect, perfect, perfect.

Except I'm cringing when he pulls into the driveway. Locking myself in the spare room to "work" when I'm not doing anything at all. Standing on the sidewalk when I got home from work, trying to find the will to open the door and be a partner.

I knew things would change, us moving in together. But I didn't think that I would change.

I missed my old life. Mara, even—she could be so sweet. One night, years before, I went out on this really shitty date, way worse than Scarf Boy. I came home and she was on the couch watching TV, and we just ate chips and she stroked my hair and it was great.

We made up. Made plans to meet her and some other

old friends at a bar. Shots happened. Like, a lot of shots happened. I looked down to check my phone at one point and there were a bunch of messages from Raph. I'd felt the insistent buzzing while I was standing at the bar, Eliza telling me all about her latest fucking ridiculous situation—some actor who stayed in character twenty-four-seven.

I didn't want to go home. I wanted to keep hanging out.

So I did.

We drank way too much, and all of us thought we were the best dancers in the world, except Mara, who never left the table. At the end of the night we were basically all crying, telling each other how much we loved each other, like so fucking much, and we need to do this more because this is what's really important, you know?

*When I finally got home, the lights were off. I figured Raph'd gone to bed, because I finally texted him on the way home—*sorry, out with the girls—*and he hadn't responded. I tried to let myself in the front door, but the door was stuck. I tried locking it, unlocking it again, but the door wouldn't move.*

Had he changed the locks?

And why the hell would that *pop into my head? Did I secretly think Raphael was the kind of guy who would do something like that?*

Crazy, right?

The door must've been broken. I went around back. I was trying to be quiet, didn't want to wake Raph, although I already planned to ask him to fix the front door—whatever was wrong with it—in the morning. I got myself a glass of water and headed for the stairs.

Stopped in the doorway—something big and bulky squatted by the front door, like a bear.

I yelped and dropped my glass. It broke. I stumbled backwards, reaching for the light switch.

No bear. No ape. Just the overstuffed velvet chair from the other side of the room. Dragged across the floor and pressed up against the front door. No wonder I couldn't open it.

"The hell?"

I left the broken glass on the floor and rounded the stairs, the elation from spending time with old friends twisting into anger. In all seriousness—

—I shoved the bedroom door open—

"What the fuck is that about?"

"Evening, darling," *Raphael said in my ear.*

I yelped and spun, shoved him. Or tried to, he barely moved an inch.

"Calm down."

"Calm down? You fucking, like—barricaded the front door! What the hell?"

"Eve—"

Yeah, so now you know why I got pissed when you called me that.

"The chair, Raph."

"I have no idea what you're talking about."

"God!" *I pushed past him. When I got to the stairwell, he hadn't followed. I motioned for him to come join me and he did, sighing and worrying at the hem of his shirt the whole way.*

Pointed at the chair. "This one."

He grabbed the chair and pulled it away from the door, then, with the most terrible scraping sound, dragged it back across the living room to its usual place.

"What chair?"

Then he went into the bedroom. I stretched out on the couch, wondering how we'd already begun sleeping in separate rooms, and how much of it was my fault, and who the fuck each of us actually was. The whole thing nagged at me. Mostly irritation at him for acting so weird. I felt a little guilty for not texting him back, and even more guilty for not wanting to. After all, I wasn't just having fun.

For the first time since we'd started dating, I hadn't missed him.

When I was a kid, I used to love Gumzys. Begged my mom to buy them for me every time we were at the store, and swiped them when she didn't. I didn't like other candy, it was Gumzys Gumzys Gumzys all the time.

Then I turned twelve, and something changed. I didn't want them anymore. They weren't bad, but the way my mouth used to water? The sheer desperate mania I used to feel when I spotted them on the top shelf?

For years I was a Gumzy girl, and then I wasn't.

When I woke up, I could smell breakfast cooking. I stumbled into the kitchen, hair sticking up everywhere. Raphael was at the stove.

"Hey," he said, waving with a spatula. "Breakfast?"

Bacon's one hell of an apology. I sat at the table and he served me, then sat with his own plate. We chatted and joked around and it all felt like the way things used to be. God, he was so handsome. Those dimples at the corner of his mouth?

And seriously, he could cook.

He drove me to work—let me pick the music, even—and we talked about seeing some new exhibition at the International Museum of Paleohistory opening that weekend. Dropped me off at my office.

Kissed me.

I was high again. Feening for Gumzys. I tried to answer emails, but I kept picturing his face. I wanted him again.

Bad.

I went into the bathroom and opened my blouse for an awkward stall selfie. Sent it off.

He texted me back right away—drooling glyph, eggplant glyph, explosion glyph—so I tried for a sexier pose and sent another one. Then Hannah came in, crying—she always went to the bathroom to cry after she lost a sale—so I slipped out, muttering it's okay and there there and all kinds of tepid shit I didn't mean.

Work was slow, so I figured I'd get Raph a present, kind of an apology gift. Sorry I was such a bitch. I logged onto Omnistock, stared at the blinking cursor in my search bar, fingers poised above the keyboard.

Then I ran to the bathroom, hoping Hannah wasn't monopolizing it with her feelings.

Thankfully, she was gone. I sank down in a stall and cried my eyes out, every blink of that cursor in an empty search box another knife to my heart.

I loved Raphael, right? Loved him. He was the person I wanted to be with.

So why couldn't I think of a single thing to buy him?

Raphael's hobbies were running, reading financial magazines, and me. He already had shoes and subscriptions. Remember when I said he didn't have any friends? This was even worse, not being able to think of anything to make him happy except what he already had. What the hell was I actually in love with? Was he even a person? Or just a smile. Dimples. Fucking abs.

My phone pinged—Raphael in the men's room, sending back a pic of his own. Gumzys all over again.

I muted my phone and got a Koach.

Twenty minutes was all it took. Most of our stuff was really his, and I was an expert in packing from the days when we used to split time between each other's apartments. This wasn't a full-on move out, more like a trial separation.

We both know what that means. But humor me, okay? I wasn't ready to leave-leave, I'd sunk so much into this thing I felt like I should want. When I packed up my makeup, Raphael's safety razor was sitting right there on the sink, and I thought about smashing it out of its plastic casing and pulling it down my wrists, one fast motion so quick I couldn't change my mind.

Since we're having this conversation you know I made it out of that house, but for this to work, you need the whole story.

The best parts of me. The worst parts of me. Hell, I'm giving you something I could never give Raphael.

Don't think that means anything.

After packing, I sat at the kitchen table with a pen poised over paper. Another blinking cursor. What could I say? How could I describe this overwhelming feeling of wrongness, with nothing real to point to? A chair?

Tears welled up again. They came hard.

A century or two later I pulled myself off the kitchen floor and texted Mara.

I wanted back into my old life, the skin I'd shed when I moved in with Raphael, and I was honestly hoping that would feel wrong too, wronger even, then I could come back with a heart full and untroubled and everything would just work.

Of course she said yes. They hadn't even filled my room, her and Kenzie. Left it a dusty monument to the chick who used to live there because they could almost afford to and you remember that year, restaurants closing down because of that cow palsy thing, and everybody was leaving the city?

There was nowhere to sleep in my old room, so Kenzie said any nights she stayed with her boyfriend, I could have hers. Convenient, except for the weird hypoallergenic covers on her pillows.

Raphael texted me. A lot.

Give me space, I replied. Like the note I never left because I couldn't think of anything to say.

He kept texting for a while, but when I didn't answer he—eventually—gave it up.

I slept in the other girl's bed and for a second

everything was put back the way it was, when I burned like a gout of wildfire, chased by boys who wore scarves in the summer and eyeliner year-round.

Boys who had Modern Love posters on their wall, Mike. Boys you sang to and moved and changed, boys you comforted in the dark, desperate nights when they laid in sweat-stained sheets with broken hearts.

Because sometimes you need to know someone else's heart can break just like yours, and it's never okay, but it is survivable.

You could call it a service, perhaps. But weren't you also feeding on their heartbreak, just a little? Because you didn't know what it was, before.

Now you do. Now we both do.

Sorry. I don't mean to be hard on you. I don't mean to be hard at all.

A month went by. I'd go two or three days without thinking about him and then it'd hit me, hard. Was I crazy? Had I blown up the best thing I'd ever had for no reason at all? Maybe I just couldn't stand being happy. What had Raphael done, even? All the texts just meant he cared. That chair thing was just to get my attention. If he was the one staying out without calling, I'd be pissed too.

He barely did anything at all, right?

The first time, I got half my suitcase packed before my stomach tightened up and I took everything back out again. Next time, I got it zipped, was about to call him, but then I realized I had an early work meeting.

Just another day or two, *I told myself. I'll text him.*

Any day now, I'm going back.

One night after work, I was lounging in my borrowed room, reading a magazine instead of calling Raphael, when Mara knocked on my door. She came in, blushing, a slight smile tugging at the corners of her mouth.

"Are you doing anything tomorrow night?"

Other than daring myself to call Raphael? "No."

"Some girls from the dance studio are coming over. After you left I started celebrating Diamet with them—"

Diamet? That hairy-legged yodeling bullshit?

"—and it's my turn to host."

"I mean, it's not really my thing."

Mara's face fell. She hung her head and rubbed a house-slippered toe against my borrowed carpet. Pouting—it shouldn't have worked on me.

Maybe I'd had my fill of disappointing people.

"Hey, come on." I gave Mara a hug. "This is really important to you?"

She nodded against my shoulder.

"I mean it'd be weird if I was just in my room, right?"

"Really?" Mara squealed. "I'm glad. I think you'll . . . you'll get a lot out of it?"

Part of me was terrified I'd start making every statement I uttered sound like a question if I lit a bunch of candles and danced around naked with Mara and her witchy friends. But what was the harm?

Maybe I'd learn something about myself.

"Diamet?" Mike said, fiddling with the sleeve of his jacket.

The sun had fallen below the mountains, just a faint orange smear across the snow-capped peaks. The temperature had dropped five or more degrees, and the night promised to grow far colder still.

"Yeah?" Evangeline said. "Why are you looking at me like that?"

"Like what?"

"It's even weirder if it's not weird to you."

"Sorry, it's just—Kara used to celebrate. It was a really big deal to her. Made up an altar and everything. I never really understood it."

"Me either."

"So what changed?" Mike gestured to the silver tantagram around her neck.

Evangeline caressed it lightly, then caught herself and stuck her hands under her hips. She rocked back and forth on the hood of the car, eyes on the mountains, not Mike.

She was quiet a long time.

Then—

"I guess that's what I'm trying to tell you."

The first thing I had to worry about was what to bring. How does one prepare for a ceremony celebrating the diurnal nature of existence? I'm not sure how much your ex told you about it, but—

No?

In the simplest terms, Diamet is about befores and afters. Not exactly change, because we're always changing. It's about the events we use to mark time. Have you ever said, "Oh, but that was before I met Zack?" Or "that was after I went to college?"

Or, this is my favorite, "that was before *the accident."*

Supposedly it's named after the ancient Terrine goddess of occurrences. The Terrines believed everything started with a semi-void, just like the Aggregationists, but instead of a universal logic dictating a void cannot remain a void forever, they believed that void contained gods. You've probably heard of most of them, like Tonans, Spiyana. Greth. Stuff they teach in the classics. So all these gods were just sitting in this void, unmoving and eternal, because the concept of things happening *didn't exist.*

And then—not one day, because they were no days— came Urda-Ek-Dia. She was the very first thing that ever happened, and birthed the concept of action, events, time itself, into life.

Immediately, the gods went to war, so offended were they that their eternal stillness was destroyed. Brother fought brother, sister fought sister, Urda-Ek-Dia above them all, uncaring of the outcome—only concerned that anything was happening at all.

The battle raged for a billion years. Eyes were put out, limbs lopped off. And worse, for the old gods could hurt in ways no human could ever conceive. Wandusk, called the Father of Wounds, tore Athelion asunder, scattering him into the void, and every luminescent hunk of skin formed a star, and look at the sky! He burns for all eternity. In revenge, Holophon cut off Wandusk's legs and speared a mighty iron stave through his chin to hold his head in place, so he might peer up at what he'd done to Athelion until the last glimmers of his mind burned out.

Amidst all this, the eldest and greatest of the gods finally noticed the one hovering above them all. Surely, she was the cause of their hardships, and if they were only to put aside their differences, they might kill her and return existence to motionless tranquility.

But first, death had to exist.

Tonans vomited forth Sulchon, god of endings—so new and small he rode on Tonans' shoulders. But he would grow quickly. Tonans and Spiyana slew Greth, the largest god of all—some say he became the Castellan range we're looking at now—and climbed his corpse until they could reach Urda-Ek-Dia, who sat in her own perfect, mocking stillness. Tonans and Spiyana butchered her, sliced her to ribbons, and then rained down hunks of flesh into the hungry gullets of their five youngest children, famished from billions of years of fighting.

As the last sliver of Urda-Ek-Dia disappeared down Nanioul's throat, the gods waited for the universe to return to complete stillness. To non-occurrence. But to their horror, they could remember a time when nothing ever happened, and all that had happened since.

They could consume her, but they could not forget

OUR BLACK HEARTS BEAT AS ONE

Urda-Ek-Dia. The Great Before, the Great After. They could never return to their state of eternal inertia.

So enraged, Tonans bound his five children—who now harbored the last essences of Urda-Ek-Dia—not with ropes or chains but their own flesh, twisting their fingers and toes together until the five could never hope to escape each other. Raquine, he called the thing he'd made from Nanioul and Fek, Karphas and Gamoa and Puez, and imprisoned them deep beneath the earth. Then Tonans retreated to his throne to slumber, an unending tribute to inaction. Not out of petulance, for now that things could be done, he was anxious to do them. No, this was his punishment, meted out by his own just and perfect hand.

After all, he was the God of Concepts. Urda-Ek-Dia could only have issued forth from him.

Before he closed his eyes forever, Tonans had one last, strange thought—maybe he had it wrong. Urda-Ek-Dia was not his issue at all, but he hers. Because this Tonans, blood-smeared and weary, was not at all the same Tonans that once sat gleaming and still at the center of infinity.

This *Tonans had been created by* her.

That's the origin. For Umber-Esoterics, Diamet is a time to celebrate the events that divide our lives. A festival of individual significance. Unlike other holidays, it doesn't occur on any kind of regular schedule. It just happens. For those who observe, we feel it in our bones, and search out others like us.

Funny—Diamet being a celebration of befores and afters. When I agreed to attend Mara's, I never thought it would prove such a potent dividing line in my own life.

I can't help but think of things in terms of before *Diamet, and* after.

The goddess at work.

I wouldn't say I was dreading *the evening, but I wasn't looking forward to it, either. On the other hand, I hadn't* spent much time with any of Mara's dance friends. I figured Diamet first, then sleep, then on the 54 bus to work I'd shoot Raphael a text to tell him I'd be home later that night. Put a foot back in that world, see how it felt, but everything would be better because I'd figured some things out.

Just don't ask me what they are.

After work, I stopped by the Truxton Market and got a bottle of wine so I wouldn't show up empty-handed at a party at my borrowed condo. When I got home, Mara was cleaning like a crazy person. I took over so she could make herself presentable. This was a big deal for her and I wanted her to have a great night. To feel good about herself. When I lived there, I mean the first time, she had friends, but she was also always the friend. Major sidekick vibes. I wasn't into chanting and lighting candles and all that shit but hey, better to be queen of something.

Around seven, the girls started trickling in. All day I'd been picturing, like, a group of spooky nuns or something. The Sisters of the Imminent Martyr. These girls were normal, like you'd find at any wine bar. This one chick Tianna definitely went to my stylist. They all kind of blended together.

Except one girl. But I'll get to her.

Eventually, Mara finished curling her hair and came out in a black velvet dress. Totally glowing. Everybody squealed and made a big show of hugging her and that just made her beam more, and I felt so good for her, like this is what she deserved, because she really was that kind of person.

Then Mara put a finger on the light switch and said, "Let's begin."

I wasn't sure what I was expecting. Maybe one of them would pull out a Tarokki deck and read everyone's fortune, and together we'd ooh and ahh over whatever deep meaning we imbued into a handful of randomly drawn cards.

But it wasn't like that, just eight chicks spreading celemans, painting their faces with daum, getting drunk and looking at pictures of Chloe's torchhound puppy. Bitching about ex-boyfriends and bosses or, in Tianna's case, her utter nightmare of an aunt. The whole thing was so horrifyingly banal. Why not call it Girls' Night? Why church it up with mystical bullshit?

That one girl I mentioned, though. Philosophee—that was actually the name her parents gave her. She went by Soph. She spent the whole night in the corner, chanting to herself, casting sullen glances at the rest of us while we, well, bitched.

Or when Tianna flashed her new fake tits, the particular before/after she was celebrating.

After the impromptu strip show, I went into the kitchen to see if we had anything harder than wine. We didn't. I shut the cabinet door and damn near jumped out of my skin.

Soph was standing there, inches away.

"Can I help you?"

She wouldn't meet my eyes, but said, "Do you know what you're celebrating?"

"This isn't my thing. I'm just here for Mara."

"Hmm. You—" She shook her head. "You think you're straddling a line, but you're already over it."

"What do you mean?" I asked, but I was kind of pissed she was being so weird.

She patted my shoulder. "Sorry."

Then she walked back into the living room, where Mara was topping off wineglasses and asking if everybody wanted to go out after.

My arm felt cold where Soph had touched me. Like pressing an ice cube to your skin. I told everybody good night, big workday tomorrow, so sorry, and disappeared into my borrowed room. Tried to sleep, but I kept feeling that cold spot on my arm, thinking about what Soph said.

Do you know what you're celebrating?

I woke up to my alarm. This was it. The day I'd put off for so long. I left before Mara got up. Texted Raph, your standard hey how're you. *Then work took over. The hours flew by and it was closing time and he still hadn't texted me back.*

I'm coming over, *I wrote.* See you soon.

The whole train ride to CG, nothing. I figured he was pissed, and had a right to be, but we'd work it out. Or maybe we wouldn't, and I'd made my peace with that, too. Why I didn't tell Mara I was leaving.

I got to the house a little after six. The lights were off, but Raph's Voigt was in the driveway. I ran a hand along the body. It really was a fine car.

At the door, I worried my keys wouldn't work, but it swung open. The house was dark and silent.

"Hello?" I called. "Raph?"

No answer.

I took a few steps into the house—not my house or our house, the house—and stepped in something wet.

"The hell?"

There was a pool of water on the floor, a small, reddish-tinged puddle.

Drip.

Droplets landed on my nose. The ceiling was discolored, swollen.

The bathroom was directly above.

I ran up the stairs, thinking—I don't know, maybe a pipe burst—but something was wrong, very wrong. My heart was hammering. I got to the top. The bedroom door was open. I called Raph's name. No answer. Everything looked the same, the bed neatly made. The bathroom door was closed, but the even thrum of a running faucet reverberated through the door. As I approached, my shoes squelched on the carpet.

I knocked. No answer.

OUR BLACK HEARTS BEAT AS ONE

Do you know what you're celebrating?

Hands shaking, I gripped the knob and pushed.

Moonlight shone through the windows, onto the clawfoot bathtub, water sopping over the sides and accumulating on the tile.

The faucet was still running.

I took a deep breath—Raphael had left the tub going, causing thousands of dollars in water damage. Dozens of jokes about men left to their own devices ran through my head. I almost laughed—how had he survived so long without me?

I splashed across the room. Cold water soaked into my shoes—the hot water heater had long since given up the ghost, apparently. Had the tap been running all day?

Just before I reached for the faucet, I noticed something on the sink. Raphael's side, a small rectangular object.

His phone.

Panic welled up in me, a voice screamed to GET OUT GET OUT GET OUT, but I was already reaching and that faucet had to be turned off, it—

The tub was filled with pinkish water.

And Raphael.

Still, pale. Dark hair covered his face like seaweed, legs folded underneath him, jagged lines down his forearms.

Of course I tried to pull him out.

Ended up in there with him, his touch colder than Soph's. He was too big, too heavy. All I could do was soak myself, splash more water over the rim.

And scream.

It's okay. It was a long time ago.

You're sweet for saying that, though.

The rest is a total blur. Flashing lights, police interviews, crackly voices over walkie-talkies. I ended up back at Mara's and we spent the night just sitting on the couch, her holding me and stroking my hair.

I found out a few details, when it was all over and Raphael was in the ground. He'd climbed into the tub about the same time we were lighting our Diamet candles, so my texts wouldn't have changed a thing. Slit both wrists with a razor. Because the faucet kept running, so by the time I found him the water had gone mostly clear.

He didn't leave a note.

I didn't know how Soph knew. But she did. My own before and after were right there in front of me and I didn't even know it.

"Shit," Mike said. "I can't . . . "

The sun was long gone, the hood cold beneath him.

Evangeline clicked the recorder off. "There. A *love lost*, everybody." She drew her legs into herself, clutching them tightly.

"I'm sorry." Without thinking he put an arm around her, and she didn't push him off, didn't shout invectives.

Just leaned into him. Soft, warm, hair smelling of something that could've been moonlight. "I spent a lot of time wishing I'd done things differently. If I'd texted him a day earlier, just a day?"

"You can't let yourself think like that."

Evangeline pulled away to look at him, a wry smirk on her face. "But I did. For a long time. Tortured myself with it. The way you have, right?"

"Kara didn't—"

"No, she didn't. But it's the same thing. If you'd said something different. Done something different. Hell, *been* someone different?"

Mike stared off into the darkness. She was right. How many conversations with Kara had he replayed, trying to find the same cracks she had?

"How did," he finally said, "how did you go from that to, uh, where you are now?"

OUR BLACK HEARTS BEAT AS ONE

Evangeline smoothed out her dress. "That's another story, and not an important one. The short version is, I wandered. Spent a lot of time on the trains, just riding. Because if I stopped moving?"

"You'd have to think about it."

"Right." Evangeline slid off the hood. "Eventually I stopped running. Started seeking. And then I found myself where you found me."

She got in the car. "We should get back."

Mike looked down at the recorder. He should've been excited, now he had everything he needed. The gaping hole in his chest felt more pronounced than ever.

Evangeline flipped down the visor, checking her makeup in the mirror. "Are you coming? I'd like to get to sleep sometime this century."

Mike cast a long look at the shadows of the mountains, a slim line in the moonlight dividing black on black. Thought about killing a god just to climb on its back and kill another.

Maybe her story had some truth to it. Maybe everything beautiful in the world was something's corpse.

He must've dozed off, because when Evangeline punched his arm, he bolted upright, a lingering sensation in his mind he'd been climbing a dead giant's spine—the skin yellowed and blackened, spongy to the touch, diseased clumps of flesh sticking to his hands while flies buzzed, buzzed—

They were parked in front of the club. All the lights were off.

"Guess this is it," Evangeline said.

"Yeah." Mike's throat felt thick. He undid his seatbelt. "Are you coming?"

Evangeline shook her head.

"I guess that's it, then." Mike got out, the sidewalk

III

swaying beneath his feet. He stuck his head back in the door. "Thanks."

Evangeline chewed her lip, then pulled a folded square of cloth from her purse. She held it out to Mike.

He took it, awkwardly. "What's this?"

"My celeman. From that first Diamet. Something to remember me by."

Mike slipped the cloth into his pocket. "You want me to remember you?"

Evangeline looked away, one hand on the wheel. Then, quietly— "What do you think of me?"

"Huh?"

"After my story. What's your, I don't know, assessment of me? As a person?"

Mike looked off down the street, trying to find the right words. "You were just living your life. And maybe you can find causality if you look hard enough, but that still doesn't mean it's your fault."

She smiled tightly. "If we kill the divine, do we kill ourselves?" she said—a line from "Liminal Gods."

Then dropped the transmission into Drive and pulled away. He watched her taillights until she rounded the corner and was gone.

Mike went into the alley. The club door was ajar. He pulled it open. The interior was dark but for a few emergency lights. He crossed the room, eyeing the bottles behind the bar. His mouth watered—god, he could use a drink—but then he drew closer. They were covered in a thick layer of dust.

"The other side of the stars," Mike muttered.

The air felt warm. Hotter still at the bottom of the stairs. He sweated under his jacket but didn't take it off. The Lady's door stood open, flashes of soft light spilling out.

This was it. The end of this strange journey. His head spun, overwhelmed by the sheer fact that over the last few days his life had been torn down to studs, built back up into something he could barely recognize.

She waited.

He went to her.

Candles burned, the swirling bank of fans chopping up their soft light and throwing it across the walls.

"Hello?"

She moved behind the fans, gliding like the shadow of a fish in shallow water. The scent she brought was incongruous, like a warm spring day, the forest after a fresh rain, flowers spewing pollen into the sky.

Redagalias.

"Where is she?"

"Evangeline? She left."

The Lady said nothing to that.

Mike fished the tape recorder from his pocket. "What you asked for. Three—"

"Stories. Good."

"What happens now?"

The shape moved behind the fans, dragging something with a great dissonant groan. Then one of the box fans in the middle row was pulled out, leaving a gaping hole like a missing tooth.

"Give them to me."

"O-okay." Mike took a hesitant step toward the fans. His hand shook. As he got closer, he buried his face in the crook of his elbow and held out the recorder, fearing something fierce and toothsome might bite into his hand, taking story and skin and bone in one barbaric gulp.

"No," the Lady said. "Just the tape."

Mike popped the tape out. "What're you going to do with them?"

"What I promised."

"Right, but—how?"

A low chuckle came from the other side of the fans. "You're not ready? Keep your stories, then, tuck them beneath your pillow. Maybe they'll keep you warm at night like *she* used to. Hearts aren't for everyone. It's perfectly normal to get along without one."

Mike ran a hand over his chest. What about those desperate, lonesome nights after Kara left? The relentless weight on his chest, pushing down on his collarbone, squeezing the life from his organs? No matter what the Lady said—and none of it was clear, not a word—what if he just went back to *that?*

"Don't worry," the Lady said. "All that pain died with your old heart. The new one will be free of such encumberments. Ready to love again. Loves like you've never known. New ways to feel and be joyful. You can't imagine it yet. But everything that comes after will dwarf all that's come before.

"Experiences are unknowable. Until you experience them."

Mike swallowed. "Okay." He reached out again.

And pushed the tape through the hole in the bank of fans.

Something brushed against him—crumbling paper, flaking off into the air. He yanked his hand back like he'd been burned.

A cracking noise on the other side of the bank, then slurping—greedy, desperate. "Mmph, mmm, mmph!"

The sound roiled his stomach, he bent over, hands on his knees, heaving.

Nothing came out.

"Guh," the Lady said, sickly smacking noises making him all the iller. "That bitch. That goddamn traitorous bitch. Ruh!"

Mike wiped his mouth on the back of his hand. "What're you talking about?"

"You . . . want this?" He could barely understand her. She sounded like she was—

Chewing.

"Yes," Mike said. "I—"

Something hit him, hard. Something unseen but heavy, it laid him out completely. He cracked the back of his head on the floor. Lights flashing in his eyes, then he was looking up at a single dangling light, flashing in time to every throb in his head.

"What?"

A figure wearing dirty grey scrubs bent over him. It also wore a mask, but not a surgical one—this mask was made from a paper plate, a man's ruddy face drawn on it in crayon. A yellow string held it around the figure's head.

"Get away!" Mike tried to sit up, but something held his hands tightly. He thrashed against his bonds.

The "surgeon" bent over him, a drawn-on grin spreading on the mask, like an animated movie.

"Calm," the surgeon said, pushing him back down.

All the fight went out of him, a narcotic warmth spreading throughout his chest. The surgeon rubbed circles between his pecs.

"There, there. A snip and you'll be done. You can head home. Back to the life you used to have. But better. We only want to make you better."

Mike's vision fuzzed. His whole body was filled with the most delicious warmth, like a shot of Josiah Blue, but turned up to eleven. In his peripherals, other shapes moved, small and bent and crooked shapes with long, stringy, greasy hair.

There was a rattling noise, one shape dragging a metal pole across the floor, a bulging bag of clear liquid taped to the top. Something pricked his arm, but he felt so warm, so distant.

The figure with the IV bag bent over him, its face the only thing that could cut through the fog.

Kara.

Not in the flesh, Kara's face was drawn on the figure's mask.

"What the fuck is this?" Mike cried. "Let me up!"

The figure's face swam, like a pebble thrown into a pond breaking up a reflection. Kara's features were gone, replaced with—

"This is better?" the Surgeon asked. "What you really want?"

"No—"

The Surgeon bent down to whisper in his ear. "All we want is to give you what *you* want. There's no grand design here. We love you, Michael."

Another figure, its mask a bizarre conglomeration of Donnie and Keegan, approached bearing a strange device, like metal jaws. Orange, two feet long with shears at the end.

And yet another, holding a silver plate. Black candles burning low.

In the middle, a wet heart, so bloody it seemed black. Crawling with tape-twined worms.

Pulsating.

"Michael," the Surgeon said again. Gnawed strands of tape, saliva-slick, dangled from its mask like tentacles.

"We are love."

A dissonant screech rent the air. The creature holding the metal jaws plunged them into Mike's mouth, pulling his own apart, impossibly wide.

The silver plate tipped, the bloody heart falling end-over-end to his lips.

Everything went black.

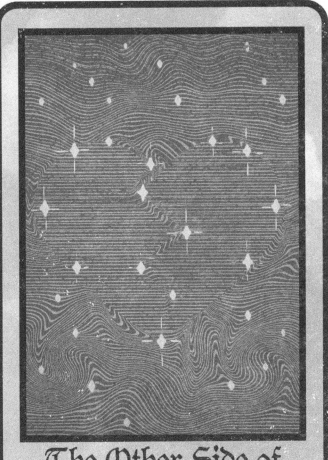

The Other Side of
the Stars

THE OTHER SIDE
OF THE STARS

SOMETHING WAS CHEWING on his shoe.

Gentle, but insistent, punctuated by little growls.

Mike opened his eyes. Found himself on a bench in Dulcette Park, near the fountains. The light felt like mid-morning. Warm, bright, casting a golden glow over the trees.

He looked down—a small brown dog happily wiggled at his feet, a pink leash hooked to its collar. The dog looked up at him, a torn shoelace in its mouth.

"Oh, Sadler! Stop!"

A woman with a partially shaved head and multiple piercings ran across the cobblestones, fountains erupting behind her. She grabbed the dog's leash. The dog looked up at her. Back at Mike, tongue lolling out of its mouth.

"Sorry. He loves shoelaces. I have to keep everything in the closet."

"It's okay." Mike snapped his fingers. The dog rolled on its belly. He gave him a scratch.

"He likes you." The woman watched him pet her dog. Then—

"I hope this doesn't seem weird. But you're the Modern Love guy, right? Mike Mallory?"

Mike patted the dog's belly one last time and stood. "I am now." He walked away, humming "Heads Are Gonna Roll" softly.

The park was full of activity. Joggers. Parents pushing strollers. Elderly couples shuffling along, holding hands.

They smiled at him when he passed.

He walked home. He should've been more concerned about the gaps in his memory—how the hell did he end up in Dulcette Park—but he wasn't. For the first time in centuries, he felt—

Fine.

Good, even.

No crushing weight on his chest, no hollowed-out emptiness, like every breath he took was being sucked down into an incomparable void. His hand still felt warm from petting that sweet little shoelace-loving dog.

He'd been through some shit, no doubt. But did it matter if he wasn't carrying it with him? Way he felt, the sun streaming down between the high-rises, was like he'd gone back in time. Before Kara, when falling in love—real love, not the furtive, sweating, grasping liaisons he'd known—was an unknown city, a place he was dimly aware of but had never visited.

He hadn't forgotten her. But now he wasn't sad or angry. Whatever happened for her, it needed to happen for both of them. She'd just gotten there first and he'd finally caught up to her. They were never going to be right.

And then he was in the Arts District, looking up at what used to be *their* building. The first time he'd stood there as a single man and not viewed the faded bricks and the rusting fire escape as irrevocably alien, spaces beyond all understanding. This was home again. Nothing to flee from.

You can't outrun anything that matters, anyway.

This could be the end. Michael Mallory, lead singer of Modern Love, pushed into a world unknown by events beyond all understanding. Hearts that once beat in time, no longer. But there's a cure for that. Michael found his, in the love of his bandmates, the falling-down streets of Benoit, the natural tension between love and obsession, because the only thing that separates them is agreement. Sucked those stories up into himself and maybe that's what made him whole. Not arcane visions of impossible surgeries, women hiding behind banks of fans. Four godlings fused together for angering their parents, the severed fifth gone forever. Not magic, not candles and chants and goddamn Diamet.

Listening.

Mike walked up four flights, ready to begin life again, and here's where it could have ended.

If Donnie hadn't been waiting outside his door.

"Where've you been, man?" Donnie said, his eyes puffy, red-rimmed. He wiped his nose with his jacket sleeve.

"What do you mean?"

"Been calling you all week. First, I figured you were off with that new girl, uh—"

"Evangeline. She's not—"

"And not like I blame you, god knows you needed that, but I figured if you were dropping out you'd, like, *tell me,* I know we don't have any more shows on the docket—"

"Donnie, what the *fuck* is going on?"

Donnie looked away. Swallowed hard.

Mike fished his keys out of his pocket. What the hell were they doing out in the hallway, anyway? Sharing their mess, whatever it was, with the neighbors instead of going in, getting comfortable, maybe raiding that bottle of Josiah in the cupboard?

"Come on." Mike stuck his key in the door. Turned.

"Me and Keegan broke up."

Mike turned back at him—like what the fuck—but he was still turning the key, pushing the door open.

A smell hit him—ashes and earth.

Then something else hit him like a ton of bricks.

The impact sent him crashing to the ground. A hulking,

grizzled man landed on top of him, knocking the wind from his lungs.

The man reared back, a knife in his hand. "*Vuschka!* What did you do to me?"

"Offa him."

The man froze. Donnie stood behind him, pressing a broken wine bottle—still sticky with pig's blood—to the man's throat, pulling his head back to better receive the blade.

Donnie yanked the man's hair. "Drop it."

"*Grotz.*" The man dropped his knife. A steel-toed boot sent it spinning across the floor, landing under the couch.

"Guess I'm out of ideas," Donnie said. "Because you're bigger'n both of us, and I'm pretty sure if I let you up, this whole thing's going to shit."

The man grunted. "Cut, then. If you can."

"You're crazy."

"No. Thought I was, these last few days." He leaned back slightly, into the meager light.

Mike gaped. "Gabrogian."

Argo Gabrogian smiled tightly. "So you remember. At least one of us does."

"What the fuck does that mean?"

The Mruatian looked at him strangely. Then the tension went out of his face, every muscle slackening at once. "My memories are all that I have. You cannot know what you've done to me."

"What're you—"

"Put your weapon away," Gabrogian said. "I won't hurt either of you."

"Fuck that," Donnie said. "You were laying up in my homie's apartment, like some fucking assassin—"

Mike held up a hand. "It's okay. Donnie, please."

Donnie scowled, but let go of Gabrogian's hair.

Gabrogian moved next, easing off of Mike. He leaned against the wall next to the door.

Mike came last, brushing himself off, his head still ringing from the tackle. He flipped on the lights and kicked the door closed.

Gabrogian stared off into the distance while Donnie paced by the couch. He set the broken wine bottle down on the dinner table, still within arm's reach.

Mike's hand went to his throat, but the flesh was smooth and unbroken. He staggered over to the cupboard and brought down the bottle of Josiah he'd shared with Evangeline.

"Three glasses?"

The other men nodded in assent.

Once served—the Mruatian eyed his for a long moment, then tipped it back, continued his slump against the wall—Donnie cleared his throat and said, "So, how do you two know each other?"

"It's a long story," Mike said.

Gabrogian smiled, a cold, lupine expression. "Stories are what've gotten us here, I think."

"The fuck's that supposed to mean?" Donnie asked.

"I think you and I are not so different."

"I doubt it."

"We share something. Or rather, a concerning *lack* of something. Am I right?"

Donnie scoffed, sat on the couch, tapping his leg.

"Memory is strange," Gabrogian said. "Mine has never failed me. I remember every battle, every scar." He pulled up the sleeve of his jacket, revealing the rough, discolored topography of a long-healed burn.

Mike grimaced at the sight. Wondered what it would be like to be hurt like that and persevere.

Despite the pain.

"But now," Gabrogian went on, "entire years, gone. I can't remember what was lost. But I remember how I used to remember." Now he fixed his gaze on Mike, those deep-set eyes boring into him. "Until I met you."

"Mike, what the hell is he talking about?" Donnie said, voice panicked.

Mike sighed, ran a hand over his chest. His new heart hammered, the persistent thrum like a bass drum, echoing in the small space of the pre-war apartment.

"I came here," Gabrogian said, eyes flicking to the sofa, the knife beneath, "to find out what you'd done to me, and how. Cut the secrets out of you, if needed. You aren't kin to the things I've hunted, but I can smell them on you. You've trafficked with them."

Mike's knees wavered, he sunk to the rug. A cold hand seized his new heart and squeezed, hunching his shoulders. There were dots to connect here.

If he had the will.

The courage.

He shut Gabrogian out of his mind, turned to Donnie. "What happened? With you and Keegan?"

"In front of *him*?"

"Don't worry about him. Tell me."

Donnie groaned, looked like he was about to spring off the sofa and go rushing out the door. But he didn't. "It's fucked, totally fucked."

"How?"

Donnie shrugged. "I don't know. That's the worst part. One day everything was fine, the next?"

"Keegan broke it off?"

"Naw, man. We *both* did. Day or two after I saw you, woke up in the middle of the night with this weird sinking feeling. Keegan called me, like five in the morning, and said some shit like *I can't do this anymore* and the fucked up thing was, it didn't feel wrong, either. I was just like *me too*. And we broke up right there on the phone. Both of us, completely done at the same time, for no reason."

Mike frowned. Nothing made sense. He always thought Donnie and Keegan's love was just like his and Kara's.

Turns out, it was. Except instead of Kara dumping him

for no reason, it was Donnie and Keegan both, each equally merciless with the other. If only it'd been that way with him and Kara. If only he'd been even a little bit done with her.

"That sucks," Mike said, "but if you were both so over it, why're you—"

"Crying?" Gabrogian said, his voice thick with wry amusement. "Your friend knows what he's lost. Knows he *should* want it, but cannot."

"But how?"

Gabrogian looked down at his hands. "Where is the girl you came with?"

He didn't know why, but Mike felt suddenly protective of Evangeline. "Leave her out of this."

"Why? That vuschka smelled of them worse than you. She's their creature, isn't she?"

All Mike could think about was the way she'd leaned into him after telling her story. Her warmth against his body. That simple, easy shared moment. "Leave her alone," he said again. "This is my fault."

"What do you mean?" Donnie asked.

What did he mean, indeed? How could he describe the strange chewing sounds when he'd handed the Lady his tape? She'd eaten it, hadn't she? Not just the tape itself, but the love transcribed within. Donnie and Keegan's, gone. Gabrogian's story of vengeance, gone.

And Evangeline's tale of loss? Was that gone, too?

If it was, had she given it with full knowledge, something the others could not? He hadn't thought much about why the woman wanted these stories, or what she might do with them.

What kind of an idiot fly lands in a spider's web and doesn't recognize it as such?

"Fuck!" Mike screamed. Spun.

Punched the wall.

His hand burst through the drywall. Flakes swirled. He didn't feel it.

He didn't feel anything.

Gabrogian had his elbow. Mike didn't resist.

"I think you know what has happened," Gabrogian said. "Some creature told you what it could do for you. But you never thought about what it might do for itself."

"She," Mike said. "She wanted stories."

The Mruatian laughed. "I knew you two were no journalists."

The bottle of Josiah reappeared. Gabrogian gave him a kitchen towel packed with ice, sat him down in a chair. The pale square on the wall where the Condaire print hung was almost indistinguishable now.

Or maybe it was the light.

Donnie huddled silently on the couch. This was Gabrogian's show, now.

"You remind me of a man I used to know," Gabrogian said quietly, "All you wanted was a salve for your own pain."

Mike nodded slowly.

"I think I know what this thing is. As much as these things can be known. It eats love. Not to feed. To destroy."

"Why?" Mike asked.

Even though Gabrogian made perfect sense.

"The Terrines believed in a Slumbering God."

Tonans. Mike flashed back to Evangeline's story. The God of Concepts punishing himself with eternal sleep for his creation, Urda-Ek-Dia, the Great Before and After. So nothing truly new could ever be introduced, just variations on a theme.

The same four chords.

"This god created every idea there could ever be, and then rested." Gabrogian kneeled on the floor, shot a hand under the couch. "Let us say, for the sake of argument, that everything the Terrines believed was true. Their gods live."

"Hold the fucking phone," Donnie said. "What's next, aliens?"

"They aren't real in the literal sense," Gabrogian said. "A lie, like all the other gods men have dreamed up. But there are things that wear such myths like clothing, so long the threads of those stories have grown into their hides. There is no difference between understanding Terrine myth and understanding these imposters. So, I ask again, how might one wake this slumbering god?"

Gabrogian stood, holding high the knife Donnie'd kicked under the couch. The blade gleamed in the low light.

"You might raise him," Gabrogian finished, "by absenting from the universe one of the ideas he'd created."

"Love," Mike said, gazing at the blade. All of it was ludicrously far-fetched and absolutely true, he could feel it in his bones. What the fuck had he done? "How do we fix this?"

Gabrogian glared at him. "Fixing is not what I do."

"Okay, so get this," Donnie said. "I can't believe I'm saying this, but if I eat something, I've got to digest it too, right? Maybe this, this thing, she's still digesting our memories."

Gabrogian considered this, or perhaps he was considering his knife. "It's a good idea. Even if we cannot get back what we've lost, I'll make sure she takes no more." He turned to Mike. "Show me where she is."

"All right," Mike said. "Just leave Evangeline out of this, okay? I think it's like you said with her. All she wanted was a salve for her own pain."

Gabrogian stared at him a long moment, then—"Fine."

The new heart in Mike's chest thumped. A reminder of what she'd given him—the Lady—and now he conspired in her murder.

If such a thing as her could be murdered.

"She's not like a real person, right?" Donnie asked. "That we're going to kill?"

"She is not," Gabrogian said, then turned to Mike. "Now, you show us."

They took the train. Mike filled Gabrogian and Donnie in as best he could. Everything he'd done and seen, including the story Gabrogian told him.

Gabrogian said little, though his eyes glinted at Mike's mention of the Rat King. Donnie just stared at his reflection in the window, overlaid on the rapidly passing cityscape.

They got off near Ehrlich Park. Mike led the others through the barren grounds. The night was still around them. Even the desperate and lonely souls who'd previously congregated around burning barrels near the edge of the park had absented themselves.

Gabrogian sniffed the air. "There's a tunnel, you say?"

"Yeah," Mike replied. "I don't know how else to get there."

"This place is ghetto," Donnie mumbled. He was wearing a black sweatshirt with the hood drawn up. His skin looked clammy, he was sweating despite the chill night air.

Up ahead, a dark shape stepped out from behind a tree.

Gabrogian snarled, knife at the ready.

"Hold on," Mike said.

The shadow stepped out into the path—skinny, long-haired, boxy glasses.

"Keegan?" Donnie shouted.

"I called him," Mike said. "Figured we should all be here for this."

Donnie eyed him. "All? What about the girl?"

Mike didn't reply. What about her? She was the Lady's creature, or close enough. He'd had a chance to turn it all over in his head on the train ride. Given what happened to Donnie, Keegan, and Argo Gabrogian, he could guess exactly what Evangeline had gotten out of the deal.

And thinking back to that night on the hood of her car,

watching the sun sink beneath the mountains and hearing the hurt in her voice, he couldn't begrudge her a little relief. Even if he wished she'd been honest about what it might cost.

"Hey," Keegan said, stopping a few feet away from them.

Gabrogian gave him a slight nod—apparently satisfied he was something that should exist, and not particularly interested in him otherwise.

Donnie rubbed his boot in the dirt, then said, "Hey. Should we hug?"

Keegan took a step towards him, then stopped himself. Wrapped his arms around his torso instead. "I'm good."

And that was it. The four of them stood there, awkward in the moonlight, until Gabrogian simply said, "The tunnel?"

"Right." Mike set off, the others falling in line behind him. Down the path through the trees, to the drainage culvert. The tunnel waited, a dark yawning mouth. He'd been swallowed up by it, once. Maybe he'd emerge again.

Maybe not.

He couldn't say what they might face, if they found their way to the club's basement again. What powers the Lady possessed, what allies might be scuttling about in the dark. But two things gave him hope.

Gabrogian—the man oozed determination from every pore.

And his friends and bandmates at his side. Even if the dynamics had changed, it didn't matter. They'd been through plenty of shit.

This was just more of it.

They gathered around the tunnel. Mike pulled out a flashlight and let the beam play over the interior. The same old broken glass, refuse, rats skittering in the dark.

"Do we just go in, or—?" Donnie asked.

"Wait," Gabrogian said, putting out a hand. He took

the flashlight from Mike, stepped into the tunnel—the glint of his knife bright as the beam. "If you're in there, come out. I would speak to you."

His words echoed down the tunnel and were not answered.

"Hold this." Gabrogian handed the flashlight to Mike, then took his knife to the tunnel wall.

"What's he doing?" Donnie asked, but Keegan shushed him.

After a few moments of scratching—nails on a chalkboard to the other three—Gabrogian stepped back, admiring his handiwork: a bisected figure eight.

A murmur drifted from the darkest reaches of the tunnel.

"You recognize it, do you?" Gabrogian shouted. "How about now?" He slashed his knife through the symbol, scarring it.

The murmurs grew louder, panicked.

"*He's come for us.*"

"*Like he came for Gamoa.*"

"*What is he?*"

Gabrogian slammed a fist against the side of the tunnel. "Come out of there, now, and parlay. Or I'll come after you."

"*He's going to kill us.*"

Gabrogian drove his knife into the dirt. He backed away. "All I want is talk."

There was a long pause, then a dry, shuffling sound, and four twisted, fused men stepped into the mouth of the tunnel. The mutilated hand of the one on the end still bled, crimson droplets splashing across broken glass.

The Rat King—

—*Raquine*—

"God! What the fuck!" Donnie cried. Keegan made a similar sound.

"Just hold on," Mike called. And even though he had no real reason to believe this, he added, "It can't hurt you."

"That's right," the man with the bleeding hand said. "Our mother and father bound us, and all our power."

"We can only cower," another added.

"Watch, wait."

"Our father sleeps forever."

"And our mother cares for naught."

As one, the Rat King said, "What will you do with us?"

Gabrogian pointed at the thing. "Names. Do not lie."

"Raquine, as one. I am Nanionul," the man on the left side said.

"Fek."

"Karphas."

"Puez," said the man with the bleeding hand. He held up the mangled appendage. "The one you killed was called Gamoa, but he was gone from us."

"Long ago," Fek said.

Gabrogian shook his head. "I wish I could remember. But the story's mine again. The boy gave it back to me." He tapped the side of his head with his index finger.

Karphas looked Mike up and down. "You're full of surprises. A most unexpected configuration."

Nanionul craned his neck. "Your friends, are they all right?"

Mike shot a look over his shoulder. Donnie and Keegan were off to the side, talking quietly, eyes on each other instead of the perverse thing in the tunnel.

That's good. That's a start.

"I suppose you seek passage again," Puez said.

"We do," Mike replied.

"And what will you do when you get there?" Karphas asked.

Gabrogian snorted. "The other's name was Gamoa, you said?"

As one, Raquine nodded.

"Then that."

"And us?" Nanioul said.

Gabrogian wrenched his knife from the earth and wiped muck off the blade. Raquine stepped back, all four constituent parts quivering.

"Your mother's the one I want." He pointed down the tunnel. "That's her, yes? The woman at the end?"

Puez said, "Not a woman, but yes. Our mother."

"And you'd give her to me, like that?"

Karphas laughed. "You might not think it a gift, when all's said and done."

"Careful," Gabrogian snarled. "My blade might still find your throat."

As one, Raquine raised its fused hands, all but the bleeding limb attached to Puez. "Or," they said, all speaking with a single voice, "it might find our bonds. You could free us, like the son of Athelion did Gamoa, so many eons ago."

"Seems like this son of Athelion had his reasons for only freeing one of you."

"It was worth a try," Fek said.

"From the story," Mike said, cocking his chin at Gabrogian, "this Gamoa—" he almost said *Volscher,* but that name didn't matter, not anymore, "—was the god of decay, I guess?"

Karphas winked. "God*ling*. And close. Entropy."

"What're you the gods of?"

"Free us and find out," Nanionul said.

"Enough," Gabrogian said. "They'll grant us passage, and we won't cut their throats. No better bargain will be struck."

"Smart," Puez said. "Some knowledge gains you nothing."

Mike rubbed his forehead. The whole conversation was exhausting, although Gabrogian showed no signs of flagging. He looked off down the tunnel, over the shoulders of Raquine. A faint pinprick of light was emerging.

"We should go." He turned to Donnie and Keegan.

Who were holding hands.

"We're, uh, not going," Donnie said.

"What?"

Keegan pushed his glasses up on his nose with his free hand. "I guess, seeing *that*—we both realized we're not really done. Something took what we had. But that doesn't mean—"

"We can't get it back," Donnie finished. They both shared a look, then turned back to Mike.

"I get it," Mike said, his previous confidence flagging, just a little. But maybe he didn't need them for whatever lay ahead. Maybe he only needed them to see what they'd seen, to realize they lived in a world beyond mortal ken, one in which the mere possibility—not probability, but possibility—their love ended unnaturally was enough to give things another shot.

Maybe they were already setting things right, all of them.

He hugged his friends, stifling the urge to go with them. But this wasn't about Donnie and Keegan, not entirely. Whatever the Lady'd done to them, she'd do to others, and if Gabrogian was right—and he seemed a man more right than wrong in most things—she wouldn't stop until love itself was gone from the world.

Then what the fuck would Mike sing about?

"Take care of yourself," Keegan said softly.

"Same," Donnie added. "Call us when it's all over and, uh, beers on us, okay?"

"Yeah."

They lingered for a moment, then went walking off through the trees. No longer hand in hand.

But they would be.

Back in the tunnel.

Gabrogian stamped and snorted about like a racehorse. "Ready?"

"Guess so."

"You have good friends. I hope this works out for them."

"Me too. We should be going."

They started down the tunnel.

"Wait!" Raquine called.

Gabrogian grunted with annoyance, but Mike turned back. The creature was mere feet away.

Eight eyes, all fixed upon him.

"Our mother is very old, and very powerful," Karphas said.

Gabrogian pointed at Puez's bloody hand with his knife. "Like this one?"

"Here," Puez said, and faster than a thing like he should be able to move, smeared his lacerated hand across Mike's forehead—warm and wet. "The blood of Gamoa still runs in our veins. We couldn't stand against Mother and Father. But we were young then. And she is alone now."

The rest chimed in then, their voices echoing in the tunnel. "You've survived many wounds. Mother is running out of ways to hurt you. Remember—"

And here they lowered their voices, four harmonizing whispers—

"There is nothing new. Not until our father awakes."

Mike touched his forehead. Rank blood stuck to his fingertips.

He should've been disgusted.

"Come," Gabrogian said, yanking on the sleeve of his jacket.

Mike followed, the voices of Raquine still murmuring at his back, too quiet to be understood.

Gabrogian glanced at his forehead and sniffed. "Their foulness is upon you."

"I'll take a shower when all this is over."

They continued on, trudging side by side through the tunnel, and unlike the last time he'd passed this way, the darkness went on forever, the pinprick of light at the end growing no bigger.

Gabrogian grew tense, his breathing hurried, his steps louder, like he was assaulting the tunnel.

"This feels like a trick. I should've slit all their throats and been done with it. Let their blood stain the ground rather than your skull."

"They're helping us."

Gabrogian stopped suddenly, grabbing Mike's collar. "Things like that do not help. They scheme and lie." He let Mike go and pushed on.

Mike hurried after him, knowing Gabrogian was probably right. How much had Raquine helped him the first time? If the thing hadn't granted him passage before, sure, he'd still be fucked up. And he wouldn't have met Evangeline—

—not that he expected to see her again—

—and Donnie and Keegan wouldn't have broken up, and maybe they'd be okay, but why should they have to go through this shit at all? Because Mike couldn't fucking go to therapy like a normal person?

Gabrogian came to a sudden stop. "How long is this tunnel?"

"I don't know. We should have been there by now."

Gabrogian turned in a wide circle, inspecting the darkness all about. "I don't like this."

Mike shot a look behind them. The mouth of the tunnel was gone, swallowed up by the ever-present darkness.

"Be ready," Gabrogian said, pressing against the wall, knife at the ready.

"What?"

A sound—rotten cloth brushing against bone. Coming from both directions. Mike shone the flashlight down the tunnel—

Something moved out of the beam.

Fast.

He squatted next to Gabrogian. "What is it?"

"Turn off your light."

Mike fumbled with the switch. Perhaps from the sweat slicking his hands, or the atavistic impulse to not give himself willingly to the dark.

"What're we—"

"No talking."

Mike huddled against the cold, corrugated metal wall, heart pounding. Gabrogian was right, they'd been betrayed. Somehow. He couldn't fathom what Raquine wanted, any more than he could the nature of the creature to begin with.

The rustling sounds grew closer—a seeming multitude—bringing with them the sickly-sweet stench of death.

A face came to him, then, pushing aside the fear, the panic. A memory. Not the one he would've thought, if his own end were at hand. Not the girl he'd made a life with, who'd thrown it away so suddenly.

Evangeline.

"I'm with you."

Gabrogian showed no sign of hearing the words. His head cocked, listening to the approaching noises.

Almost upon them, now. Maybe Gabrogian intended to lie quiet, hoping whatever made them would pass by. A foolish thought—surely whatever approached knew every shard of glass, every puddle, every spot of rust on the walls.

Surely, they sensed two warm bodies in their midst.

Something brushed against Mike's foot. He stifled a yelp, yanked it back. Something else touched his hair. They were all around, now, crawling on the walls, the ceilings—

"Ruh!" Gabrogian yelled, lunging. He collided with an unseen shape, hitting the opposite wall, a puff of rancid dust filling the air.

Bony fingers wrapped around Mike's wrist. He swung the flashlight, it cracked against something, but it let go of his wrist. He flipped the light on, illuminating his attacker.

OUR BLACK HEARTS BEAT AS ONE

At first, he thought it was a bundle of soiled rags, but nestled within the rotting deathshroud was a face of yellowed bone. Mud dripped out of its three eye sockets, worms writhing in the morass. The thing's jaw, speckled with a handful of broken teeth, hung loose, more worm-shot mud dripping from its open mouth.

Mike shoved it back, whirled to run, but another creature blocked his path. Something crashed behind him—Gabrogian, fighting.

Hopefully winning.

The creature reached for Mike. He batted its hand away with the flashlight and darted past. Bony fingers raked his back, tearing through his shirt, each slash like a lightning strike.

He ran towards that hopeless pinprick of light at the end of the tunnel. Hands reached for him, tearing away bits of cloth and skin.

Behind him, Gabrogian bellowed.

Then wailed.

The sound pierced his eardrums. He felt sick. The fuck kind of person was he, anyway? Dragging Gabrogian into this, then leaving him in a tunnel for these, these—revenants? As good a word as any—to tear asunder?

No wonder Kara left him. Peel back the music, the ragged rock vagabond clothes, the boozy swagger? What was left?

What the hell was Michael Mallory, anyway?

Dammit.

Mike staggered to a halt, turned. A revenant lunged at him. He swung the flashlight again, catching it under what little chin remained. The skull whipped back with a resounding *crack* that echoed down the tunnel. Dropping low, Mike kicked out its legs, brittle bone snapping. The thing went down. Mike smashed it with the flashlight once, twice, the skull breaking apart into jagged fragments. A worm-ridden glob of mud lay at the center.

He reared back and stomped it apart with his boot.

Mike aimed the flashlight back down the tunnel. The passage was jammed with revenants, tripping over each other to get at him. He couldn't see Gabrogian.

Just a swarm of old bones, animated by clumps of earth.

Coming for him.

"Yes!" Nanioul's voice drifted down the tunnel. "The Necrophim are distracted, my brothers!"

"Our chance!"

Mike's heart pounded. His *new* heart. He gripped the flashlight tightly, the army of the dead shuffling towards him, step by awkward step.

He realized he was singing. Had been for some time. Maybe it started as a familiar tune, "Heads Are Gonna Roll" or "Liminal Gods," but it morphed into something else, something unsung and unheard and, though he hadn't planned anything of the sort and never thought he would after that moment in his apartment when he gambled, sang "Eve," and was damned—

For *her*. A single lyric, pregnant with all the power of his craft and his forebears, echoing back to the moment some human pre-cursor spent a single second of their existence not just surviving, fucking, or sleeping, but doing something *else:*

—No matter what we've done
Our black hearts beat as one—

Everything slowed. His words, his pulse, the revenants. The mark on his forehead burned.

Ice-cold, hell-hot, all at once. He dropped the flashlight, the beam spinning as it fell. Bent over at the waist, the pain immeasurable, searing his skin—

I guess there's magic in you, after all, Evangeline whispered, deep inside his mind.

And then Gabrogian, louder, gruffer, deep voice accusatory, finger pointing at Mike from nowhere—

Their foulness is upon you.

The mark! The blood of Gamoa.

Time sped back up. The revenants, illuminated in the fallen beam of his flashlight, pushed forward, shoulder to shoulder. Bone scraping bone.

Mike rifled through his pockets, hand brushing against satin. Evangeline's celeman, the one her friends gifted her on that first, fateful Diamet. He pulled it out quickly, spat on it, and wiped his forehead, scrubbing hard.

The burning stopped.

Mike bunched up the celeman and tossed it down the tunnel. As one, the revenants' heads turned, tracking the item. It fell in a dirty puddle.

The revenants fell upon the celeman, ripping it apart, shoving each other aside in their fury. They tore it down to strips, to scraps, to atoms. Fighting over every last bit.

And when it was gone a great wail went up from the creatures that made Mike's heart twinge, for their only purpose had been satiated and now there was nothing left for them in creation, or anywhere beyond. Then they, bones and shrouds and all, collapsed into dust, and a wind came hurtling through the tunnel and blew it all away.

"Fuck." Mike stooped and picked up his flashlight, pointed it back down the tunnel. "Gabrogian?"

Silence.

Mike stood there, unsure what to do. The other man could be hurt, or worse. He cast a glance over his shoulder. What had been a pinprick of light was now clearly the tunnel exit, the streets of that unknown and unknowable part of the city—if that's what it was—visible through a thin, gauzy mist.

He could go on, without Gabrogian. But what chance could he stand alone?

If he even *was* alone, because Evangeline had been with him, for a moment.

Hadn't she?

Footsteps rang out from the other side of the tunnel. Gabrogian, disheveled and mud-smeared, lurched towards him, knife held low at his side.

Blood dripped from the blade.

"I found our friend," Gabrogian said. "Trying to crawl out of the tunnel. I should've trusted my judgment the first time."

Mike pictured four throats, slit clean in a line. Four bodies fallen in a pile, the flesh fused together.

Gabrogian reached him, looked him up and down, gaze lingering on Mike's forehead. "Just remember. Their *gifts*?

"No gifts at all."

The strange part of the city, or the strange part of no city at all, was deathly quiet, but for the howl of the wind. After the grit and grime of the tunnel, his skin scoured by the dusty touch of the revenants, the breeze felt good. Clean. Pure.

The slashes on his back had stopped bleeding of their own accord. Outside the tunnel, the Mruatian stripped. His hairy body was covered in cuts. One on his arm, nestled amidst several pale-white scars, was deep, the jagged flesh flapping, blood gushing. Gabrogian tore his shirt into strips and bound the wound.

He caught Mike staring. "I've had worse." He tied the shirt-strip off with a grunt and put his jacket back on, zipping it up over his naked belly.

They walked side-by-side up the middle of the street. The buildings around them were dark.

"You did well back there," Gabrogian said.

"Really? Thought I was just screaming a lot."

"You found your own way to end them. All that matters." They spoke no more until they arrived at the club. They'd still seen not a single person, not a single car. Not even rats feeding on the leavings of men.

Nothing.

The club itself was not only closed, but boarded up. Broken glass crunched under Mike's feet. He turned to Gabrogian.

"Maybe she's gone."

"This isn't a place." Gabrogian sniffed the air. "It's her. All her."

"What do we do?"

Gabrogian walked up to one of the boarded windows, reared back, and kicked the plywood. The board fell from the window frame with a loud *crack* that resounded down the empty street like a gunshot.

They waited, heads swiveling, for something to happen. Nothing did.

The Mrautian drew his knife and entered.

Mike thought about letting him go. Maybe he'd done enough—this was Gabrogian's specialty, not his. He wrote songs. A poet, not a warrior.

Donnie's face came to mind, unbidden. Pale, haunted, skin stretched to the point of breaking.

Me and Keegan broke up.

Mike set his jaw and followed Gabrogian into the dark heart of this uncanny hell.

Inside, for the third time. The interior was overgrown with cobwebs, the floor littered with dry, crackling leaves. A dark shape lay face-down in the middle of the dance floor. Too small to be Gabrogian, who was nowhere in sight.

Mike looked about uncertainly.

Strange—just a week ago, he couldn't have imagined being in mortal terror of his own life. He would've welcomed it, and all the possibilities the clenching feeling in his chest intimated. Maybe he hadn't quite settled on a reason yet. But something within him wanted to live.

And even though the Lady Behind the Fans required

an ending, a silent part of him would always be grateful for what she'd done.

Mike approached the body on the dance floor, kicked it over with his toe. Male, young. No one he recognized, but he could've easily been in the audience at a Modern Love show. The man's skin was bleach-white, drained of blood. Eyes open and staring at Mike. Mouth open, too, teeth removed and blood dried over his empty gums.

Simultaneously, both his hands opened, revealing a mess of teeth clutched in either palm.

Who this boy was, how he'd come here, how he'd died, none of it mattered. This was a gift from the universe, that usual master of obfuscation, nuance, misdirection. Hard evidence Mike trod the righteous path, and whatever he did from here on out was justified.

Mike left the corpse behind. The basement door was open, yellow light spilling out.

A faint crash echoed through the doorway. Mike followed the sound, down the steps yet again. Through the hallway at the bottom, into that familiar room.

Crumpled forms littered the floor, each wearing a paper plate mask and lying in a spreading pool of blood. The fans were knocked over, some still spinning, others halted, their cords pulled from the walls. Gabrogian stood amidst them, hunching over, a look of intense concentration on his face.

Mike's heart—his new heart—throbbed, electric black pulses traveling his bloodstream, obscuring his vision.

Then he was running, hurling himself at the Mruatian.

Gabrogian spun and backhanded Mike, his teeth snapping together, sending him flying across the room. He cracked his head against the wall. His heart pounded, a drumbeat summoning him back to war, but his body would not heed the call.

"Don't get up," Gabrogian said. "I must work." He bent down, his arm working back and forth in a rhythmic motion.

Sawing.

Wet sounds came from the Mrautian's effort, dark ochre splattered his face. Finally, he bolted upright, a round object held in one hand, ever-bloody knife in his other.

"Ha!"

Gabrogian turned to Mike, eyes burning like twin coals. He hefted the object in his hand, then tossed it between Mike's splayed-out legs.

"Here is the thief that thought herself a god."

Mike, who knew he shouldn't look, who didn't need another horrible thing rocketing up from the depths of memory every time he closed his eyes—

Looked.

That the "Lady" sobriquet was a misnomer went without saying. Something dwelt behind the fans, and paced and spoke and made terrible deals with broken-hearted musicians, but nothing of it was aristocratic, or even womanly. The thing at Mike's feet—her head, must be—was dark purple, bulbous, hairless, misshapen, coated in some sort of mucus. Looked more like a hunk of diseased muscle. So strange was the thing he couldn't tell where Gabrogian had sawed it off the body. If he stared long enough, and he did, his mind conjured the alien topography of her features into something resembling a face, eyes and nose and mouth, but it was the sort of intellectual alchemy one might use to transform a cloud into a dog or a car.

Or a mountain, into the bones of a god.

Mike's stomach lurched, he turned from the sight and heaved. Nothing came up but bile, burning his throat, watering his eyes. He pushed himself up the wall until he was standing.

His heart spasmed. Electric pulses caressed his mind.

Don't worry, dear. The best part of me is still within you.

Perhaps I should call you *mother.*

The word echoed in his head, over and over—*mother, mother, mother.*

Gabrogian approached, kicking the Lady's head off into a dark corner. He looked bored.

"Her children put up more of a fight."

Mike swallowed deeply, feeling sick. "I guess that's it, then." He laid a hand over his chest, knowing it wasn't, could never be.

"One last thing."

"What?"

Lightning quick, Gabrogian snatched up the lapels of his jacket, pulling Mike towards him.

The knife entered Mike's chest a millisecond later.

"Sorry," Gabrogian grunted, twisting the knife, slicing through muscle. "I told you my charge was eliminating things from the world which shouldn't be. You—" he grunted again, "—carry such a thing."

Mike tried to fend Gabrogian off but couldn't make his arms work. His limbs went numb.

Then the pain came—burning, grinding, blinding.

He screamed. The Lady screamed with him.

Until Gabrogian laid a hand on his shoulder and wrenched his knife free. Speared through was Mike's false heart, a black knot of muscle, crawling with worms.

"I'm not your killer," Gabrogian said softly. "You died the moment you chose to truck with black magic."

Mike crumpled to the floor, dimly aware of the gaping hollow in his chest where a heart used to be.

Gabrogian tipped his knife down. The heart slid slowly off the blade, hitting the floor with a soft *spluch*. Then he reared back, stomped it with his boot. Again and again and again.

Mike had just enough time to wonder how he, heartless, could still watch the destruction of his extricated organ.

Then he wasn't watching anymore.

OUR BLACK HEARTS BEAT AS ONE

The room seemed familiar, but his hazy mind couldn't quite place it. Black walls. Candles in silver sconces. A tantagram carpet stretched across the floor.

In the middle, Evangeline sat on a leather couch, tarokki deck splayed out on the coffee table in front of her. She gazed at the cards, brow furrowed.

Then looked up.

Smiled.

"Sorry about that," she said. "Didn't mean to scare you. I just thought, you know, it'd be better if you saw it for yourself. More believable."

Mike gaped at her, then looked down at his own chest. Ran a hand over it. No wound. "How—"

Evangeline waved a hand over the cards. "Another reading, like before. I had to show you what was going to happen."

"Going to happen? So, all that, the basement, Gabrogian—"

"You're still in the tunnel."

The tunnel. Images of revenants, eye sockets dripping wormy mud, popped into his head.

"All things being equal, this isn't the worst outcome. The things *she* made me do, all for a promise she never intended to keep? If your death's the price that must be paid for her end, well, it'd mean something at least." She stood, crossing the room quickly, taking his hands in hers.

"But I'm not willing to pay it."

She leaned forward. Electricity shot through Mike's limbs. Everything slowed, his heart thudded.

Then her lips found his.

It was like the first kiss. Not *their* first kiss, which it was, but the first kiss in history, that inaugural moment when two humans thought to try *this*, a campfire burning bright behind them, predators howling in the distance.

The Aionic *Ideal* of a kiss. The ur-kiss. The purest example of its breed, springing fully formed from the brow of Tonans, slumbering god of concepts, creator of everything there could ever be.

Mike didn't want to pull away.

Eventually, Evangeline did, eyes sparkling in the candlelight. "I'm sorry I was—the way I was. When I first saw you, you were just a way to get all this terrible shit out of my head. Ten years doing that bitch's dirty work, then you come along, and it's like here's her promise. I thought I wanted all that shit with—I can't remember his name now, out of my head. And she gave me that. You gave me that. And when it was gone, I realized I'd been running on pain alone, for years. Faster and faster and then you take it away and it's like I hit a wall. But then I dusted myself off, and what I do remember, the stuff I didn't let her take? You heard the worst of it and you didn't look at me any different. I got done spilling my guts and you, what do you do?

"You put an arm around me.

"You don't judge me, and you sure don't try to fuck me. You take all this goddamn baggage that's been dragging me down and it goes into a tape recorder and then you're still there? Here's what I'm trying to say. I'm not good at this, but—

"I fucking love you, Michael Mallory. I love you."

The moment hung there, in between them, ready and willing. All he had to do was seize it.

"Evangeline, I—"

He couldn't finish.

He knew the words, he just had to say them, but his tongue felt like clay in his mouth. His heart beat dully, like the simple organ it was. Diligently delivering blood throughout his body, unconcerned with its second—or perhaps primary—and most esoteric, poetic function. Mike pulled away, dropping his head. Ready to be delivered back to Gabrogian's knife and will.

OUR BLACK HEARTS BEAT AS ONE

The whole errand had been a lie. Why would that creature create more of the thing she so wanted to absent from the world?

His heart was gone for good.

Something he'd known, the moment Kara left. Love left him that day, too—the concept, like a Terrine god taking wing, crashing out the window, hurtling up into the night, just a shadow-smear across the moon and then gone, gone—

"Hey." Evangeline grabbed his chin, turned his face toward hers. "It's what she gave you, isn't it?"

Mike nodded.

She ran a hand down his chest. "I always figured that part was a lie. An approximation, something to let you blend in." She sighed. "One thing I learned, all those years, laboring under the weight of my own guilt. There's no easy answers." She wiped away tears, grinning through them anyway. "Might sound strange, considering I conned you into sucking some bad memories out of my head, but everything I had to do to get there?

"Maybe someday I'll tell you."

"I'd like to hear that," Mike said, and meant it.

Something twinged inside him.

Evangeline looked at him curiously. "There's something there. A fragment. We can build off that."

"What?"

"Listen," she said quickly, "this isn't something someone can just give back to you. It's something you have to make yourself."

"I don't understand."

She grabbed him by both arms. "I think you do. That bitch is a trickster, but she told you everything you needed to do. Gather stories? Except she didn't tell you what you *really* had to do with them. Not record them for her. Listen to them. That's how you reforge your heart."

"Listen to them?" He closed his eyes, let the stories he'd heard wash over him. The shit at the core of them, too.

Keegan and Donnie, they just worked, and they didn't poke too hard at the whys, because they didn't need to.

Argo Gabrogian's tale, that story was only half Gabrogian's. The other half, Moston, the man Mike never met? Consumed by grief, but willing to do *anything* to avenge his love. Even go toe-to-toe with a god. By proxy, but still.

And Evangeline. Her and Raphael—an imperfect love, perhaps the Aionic Ideal of such. But real, nonetheless. That feeling of looking down the cold dark corridor of the future, knowing you're fated to walk it alone, without the one you chose at your side?

Same as his. Less blood, but the end result was the same.

Endings are far more palatable when there's at least the pretension of mutually agreed dissolution. Him? Evangeline?

They both suffered the same wound.

Something stirred within him. A faint pulse, so slight and deep he wouldn't have noticed it if he hadn't been looking. A seed, stretching and growing, pushing aside the worm-ridden dirt atop it. Straining, implacable, demanding its moment in the sun, and all the nourishment it would provide.

His heart thrummed, dark electricity crackling up his body, a voice hissing invective in the back his mind—

But fainter, fainter. Like it was bleeding out.

Then the hiss became a gag. A death rattle.

"Evangeline."

She embraced him, and he her, pressing their bodies against each other so fiercely it was like they were trying to meld themselves into a single being, hearts beating in time to a song of revivification.

Bringing him back to life.

Not mouth to mouth.

Heart to heart.

OUR BLACK HEARTS BEAT AS ONE

Tha-thump.

Tha-thump.

Warmth bloomed in his chest. Something inside him broke, in the best possible way.

The words came on their own, words he thought he'd never speak again, spilling from his mouth in a joyous tumble:

"I love you, too."

They stood like that for a very long time. Entwined, like Raquine. Still, like the elder Terrine gods before Urda-Ek-Dia ruined the party.

And happy. Like none of the above.

We could leave them like that. They've earned it, yes? And you could, too. Close the book. Put it down. Burn it, if you must. You are your own god of endings. When you stop, they'll stop, too. *Happily ever after* could be a permanent embrace, in a living room bathed in candlelight, tarokki cards splayed across the table. This could be the future, and beyond, if you will it.

But you don't.

The fucked up thing about happiness? We all say we want it. We dream of it. Beg for it. But it doesn't satisfy, does it? It's an empty meal. Leaves us hungry.

You seek satiation?

Keep on.

The squirming started in his chest. Light, feather-strokes across his organs. Then traveling up his throat, harder now, writhing, scoring the flesh.

Evangeline reached for him. "Are you—?"

Mike turned and vomited all over the tantagram on the floor, a long, violent geyser out of black, viscous discharge. It burned. He wiped his mouth on his sleeve.

A mass of worms wriggled on the floor, crawling all over each other. He felt sick, ready to vomit once more.

That had come out of him? Their stench filled the room, iron and death.

"Sah-halik!" Evangeline cried. The tantagram on the carpet spun, losing its shape, then burst out of the fabric, the white lines of the design three-dimensional now, enclosing the wormy mass like a bear trap and sucking it back into the carpet.

Evangeline gave him a hand towel. "Why I told you not to piss yourself on it."

He wiped himself off, casting sidelong glances at the now-still tantagram. He wouldn't be sitting on it again.

"God," he managed, his voice a wheeze. He bunched up the towel and looked about for a place to put it.

Evangeline motioned to the trash can beside the sofa, then passed him a glass filled with dark liquid.

He sipped—wine. Good wine. It washed away the acrid taste.

"Her gifts? No gifts at all."

But this last was said not with Evangeline's voice, but Gabrogian's. The room faded, Mike reached for her, but his arms wouldn't move, and she was receding, her hand open and angled in such a way that if he really wanted to believe it?

She was reaching back.

Again, the tunnel. Mike holding his flashlight, Gabrogian gripping a bloodied knife, the tunnel's mouth opening up on the strange part of the city, cobblestones dewy from a recent rain.

Mike stuck the flashlight under his arm and rubbed his eyes. He felt woozy, punch-drunk, whipping back and forth between past and future.

If any of that had even happened. A hallucination, brought on by blood loss—couldn't the wound on his back be worse than he thought? It could.

OUR BLACK HEARTS BEAT AS ONE

Many things could be worse than he thought.

"Well?" Gabrogian said.

"Just—give me a minute." Maybe he'd imagined it all. Maybe he hadn't.

Maybe, just maybe, there was a way to tell.

Mike shut his eyes. Let his mind go blank, let the tunnel and the Mruatian and the stench of blood drift away. Even the burning slashes on his back. And when it was all gone, when he drifted in an endless, soundless void, nothing above and below and, most importantly, nothing within—

He thought of her. Her face, filling his mind's eye. Lighting the darkness.

His heart responded as it should. Beating faster, lighter, fluttering around in his chest like a hummingbird.

He knew what was real.

Mike opened his eyes.

"Are you hurt?" Gabrogian asked.

"Not anymore." Mike glanced at the mouth of the tunnel, the darkened streets beyond. A world he'd blundered into, like a wounded animal falling into a ravine. He should've known nothing there could help him.

Except Evangeline. And they'd pulled each other out into the light. Bound each other's wounds.

He thought about Donnie and Keegan. Their love wrenched away. The resolute looks on their faces as they walked away into Ehrlich Park, amongst the dying trees. That prevaricating thing in the basement might've taken their love. But she couldn't take their faith.

A more powerless creature he couldn't fathom.

They'd be okay. Everyone would.

"I'm sorry I dragged you into this," Mike said. "I could say I didn't know what I was doing, but—" he shrugged, "—here we are."

"No. You must show me—"

"You'll find it. And when you do, I honestly don't care what happens. Here." Mike held out the flashlight.

Gabrogian took it. "How will you find your way back?"

"I've got a light at the end."

Mike turned back to the darkness. A faint pinprick of light shone at the opposite end, for him and him alone. He took one step, then another—

Gabrogian grabbed him by the jacket and wrenched him around, muscling him up against the tunnel wall.

Mike held his hands out at either side. "Let me go."

"If you won't help me, I won't wait any longer. There's something unnatural inside you. I'll have it out." Gabrogian raised his knife.

"Hey, what the fuck are you doing? It's not in me anymore, okay? We got it out, we—"

Love is your armor, Evangeline whispered in Mike's mind. *Strong as he is, he's no match for you.*

"It's nothing personal," Gabrogian said.

And, again, plunged the knife into Mike's chest.

It passed through skin, muscle, bone.

Without leaving a mark.

Gabrogian pulled the knife back—clean—and frowned. "What?" He tried again, and again, with the same result. The blade passed through Mike like he wasn't there at all, like Gabrogian was stabbing the fog.

"Stop," Mike said, grabbing Gabrogian's forearm and pushing him away. The Mruatian kept looking from his blade, to Mike, with puzzlement.

"How—"

Evangeline spoke to him then, and Mike relayed her words, every single one. A song, a duet, a perfect, psychic harmony:

"The things you hunt, the things you kill? You said it yourself. They're all the same, and they're not complex. *Things of teeth and claws?* They're all out to take something from us. You understand them implicitly. That's your power over them.

"This is something you can't understand. You can't kill.

Accept that, and you'll be happier. Go, and seek the winged, the toothed, the things that run wild when the moon burns blood-red in the sky, because no matter how much you hate to admit it, you and they dwell on the same side of the stars. What's in our hearts does not. You'll never reach it."

Gabrogian screamed, his voice resounding off the tunnel walls. His body shook, a violent quake that seemed fit to break the man apart.

Then he turned and spat. Slipped his knife back into the scabbard at his belt. "Vuschka."

"You're one of them, aren't you?" Mike said. "That's why you hate them so much—" and a name came to his lips, out of the ether, or out of memory, "—Sulchon?"

Gabrogian eyed him for a long moment, then stalked away, out of the tunnel, into the strange part of the city. To do what he would.

Mike brushed himself off, fingers lingering over his chest. He turned and headed back down the tunnel. His foot brushed against something large and substantial, but it made no sound, no movement, and he left it behind.

Outside the tunnel, the sun had come up. Ehrlich Park was silent around him, a light breeze fluttering the bare branches. He didn't know what time it was, how he'd get back. Maybe he'd walk, like before, on those lonely, desperate nights when he needed so badly to keep moving just to stay alive.

At least now he was walking towards something.

When he exited the park, he spotted a dark car waiting at the curb beneath a shattered streetlight, a figure sitting on the hood.

Evangeline climbed off the car. "Hey, you."

Mike ran to her, swept her up in his arms. They kissed, bodies pressed tightly together, and this kiss was the same as the first. All-consuming.

Everything.

Mike finally pulled away and looked at her. She was wearing a Modern Love shirt. He twisted a bit of fabric in his fingers. "Looks good on you."

"It'll look better off," Evangeline said, throwing open the driver's door. "Come on. Let's fucking go."

Mike climbed in, not looking back at the desolate park behind him.

His true heart fuller than he ever dreamed it could be.

A year later, they stood on the observation deck of the Cobb Building at sunset, arm in arm. Ordinarily the platform would be packed with tourists, all jockeying to get a glimpse of the sun dropping into the river. They'd been cleared out hours before, at no small expense. But with "Our Black Hearts Beat As One" climbing the charts and the ink on their deal with TRG/Anti-Scope barely dry, the boys from Modern Love could afford all kinds of things.

Even a wedding like this.

Things hadn't always been easy since that last night in Ehrlich Park, but they'd been good. Mike moved out of the old pre-war apartment and into a loft down the street from the Beacon. He and Donnie spent a weekend sound-proofing the place, and now they had a reliable practice space in the city.

As a bonus, it was only a few blocks from Evangeline's.

In the first few weeks, as all the emotions and strangeness faded, he worried their feelings for each other might fade too. But their passion burned brightly as ever, brighter still with every kiss and caress, every late night entwined in each other's arms, spilling their deepest, darkest secrets.

At least those they hadn't yet spilled.

They argued, on occasion, but never about anything consequential, and even in disagreement, they never lost sight of the regard each felt for the other, or the choice they'd made.

OUR BLACK HEARTS BEAT AS ONE

Never quite shrugged off the darkness, either, but they were haunted people and still they loved each other for it.

A few weeks after moving into his new place, Mike had been down at the Truxton Market, picking up wine for dinner. He'd been paying for the bottle when some strange impulse told him to turn around. He obeyed, looking out across the market, at the throng of shoppers and vendors.

And saw her.

Kara's hair was different, shorter. She'd pierced her nose, too. She was at the flower stand, sniffing a bouquet of redagalias, a canvas shopping bag slung over her shoulder.

He studied her face for a moment, decided she looked happy, and turned away before she caught him staring.

"You know the Terrines didn't have a god of love?" Evangeline said.

Mike wrenched his gaze away from the people on the riverwalk below, just tiny specks. "No?"

"One for practically everything else. Makes me think."

"About what?"

She pulled him away from the railing, looking into his eyes. "Maybe love doesn't come from the divine. It's from . . . somewhere else. Something above gods. Beyond them."

"Maybe." He kissed her, not as long as he would've liked, because just then the music started up.

Mike rolled his eyes. "I like Martyrcycle as much as the next guy, but at a wedding?"

"They're your friends," Evangeline said with a smile, because that wasn't really true anymore, she was as much a part of Donnie and Keegan's life as Mike was.

They took their seats, the sun disappearing behind the far riverbank. Donnie and Keegan traded vows and when they kissed, Evangeline leaned her head on his shoulder and maybe every day couldn't end perfectly.

But this one did.

CODA

THE LADY GOT her three stories, sure, but there's only one that matters.

Loves lost, loves avenged? Dirty, desperate men all in a row? Capricious women, narcissistic men? Swirling fans and the powers that hide behind them, feeding on emotions they'll never feel themselves?

No.

The only story that matters is that of two broken people, wounded, blood-leaking creatures, stumbling about with no purpose other than to flee the pain that's everywhere, surrounding them, hiding inside the membranes of every cell, eating them from the inside out.

The ones they loved before, and lost? They thought their love was a mirror. But that was a lie. Or at best a distortion, an overly generous and absurdly willful interpretation.

These two? Their love isn't a mirror. Their *pain* is, and they are each the other's bandage.

Together, they stopped the bleeding.

But after the pain's gone, what then? Pain gives life meaning. Purpose. Without it, you just have to exist.

And how fucked up is that?

Mike and Evangeline, maybe they'll keep existing together. Or maybe one day they'll wake up, see the other as nothing but a blood-soaked bandage, and make their exit. And because of the blessed circumstances under which they met, they won't go through anything approaching what they did before.

They can't bleed like that again.

Maybe this works. Maybe it doesn't. We're pulling the curtain, now. Mike and Evangeline, together forever. Or soon to part.

Choose the ending you prefer. That's more grace than any of us get.

END

MODERN LOVE SONGbOOk

Heads Are Gonna Roll
(Lyrics by M. Mallory, Music by M. Mallory/D. Fremont/K. Taylor)

Verse 1
You in your skintight dress and your black lipstick
Lord knows you're dressed to kill
And the bars are playing requiems
for the blood about to spill
This whole damn night's an upturned throat
Just beggin' for a knife
And you were born a switchblade
Who can't help herself but slice

Bridge
Baby listen . . . there'll be no mercy tonight . . .

Chorus 1
'Cause heads are gonna roll!
(From the minute that you stepped in)
Yeah heads are gonna roll!
(You're brandishing your weapons)
Heads are gonna roll!
(There'll be no peace no quarter)
Heads are gonna roll!
(Get ready for the slaughter)
Yeah heads are gonna roll . . .

Verse 2
On past the bar there's the killing floor
Where you're sizing up your victims
Drunk on booze and heat and youth
They'll never know what hit them

BRIAN ASMAN

Lick your lips and twist your hips
Under the flashing lights
Your claws are sharp, your teeth are bared
It's a massacre tonight

Chorus 2

Outro (spoken)
My lady, on your throne of bones
Picking flesh from your teeth
I crawl through carrion
To lay prostrate at your feet
Do what you will

Egomancy
(Lyrics by M. Mallory, Music by M. Mallory/D. Fremont/K. Taylor)

Verse 1

Life isn't really quite the shape
You always thought that it would take
They cut you once, they cut you twice
You've been bleeding all your life
They buried you here part by part
In this graveyard of broken hearts
But maybe there's enough body left
You can find a way to resurrect

Chorus

It's not alright
You cry out to the night
And no one's there to listen
No one's there to listen
If you need some help
To conjure up yourself
I might just have a notion
I may just have the notion

Verse 2

You're reeling from another blow
Wishing you could take control
These days the beatings never end
You dust it off, get clocked again
This isn't who you oughta be
But the years ticked by so viciously
What happened to that upright man?
Who held the world in his two hands?

Chorus 2

Bridge
*The magi fall silent
But that isn't so tragic
If the grimoire's blank
Make your own kind of magic*

Chorus 3

Outro
*I need a potion
I need a tincture
Some kind of elixir
There's blood on the speakers
Tell me a story
Sing me an anthem
Mutter a mantra
Tell me I'm handsome
Tell me I'm okay
Tell me I'm okay
Tell me I'm okay
Tell me I'm okay*

Our Black Hearts Beat as One
(Lyrics by M. Mallory/E. Cash, Music by M. Mallory)

Verse 1
Once you wanted to share my name
Now they call you the winter
But I'm the one who's frozen in place
I thought our love was a mirror
The reflection looks so strange
Twisted beyond our darkest dreams
Is that really you and me?
And are we still anything?

Chorus 1
And we fled from their knives
Gave ourselves back to the night
Prowled these darkened streets
Broken glass beneath our feet
So what if hope is dead
We can't hurt like this again
Through all the evil that we've done
Our black hearts beat as one

Verse 2
Once we wanted to build a home
Now it's falling to pieces
I loved you right down to the bone
And I just can't believe it
There's a stranger in this house
For the life of me I can't tell
If it's you or me
And are we still anything?

Chorus 2
And we fled from their knives
Hid ourselves away from the light

BRIAN ASMAN

Lost on these nameless streets
Numb to every melody
So what if hope is dead
We can't hurt like this again
Through all the evil that we've done
Our black hearts beat as one

Verse 3
Now we've found a place to bleed
Fancy meeting you here
You and I were cut the same
Our wounds are a mirror
We can staunch them if we try
Take turns with the sutures
Is there a you and me?
Can we be something?

Chorus 3
And we survived their knives
Lit a fire in the night
Learned to love these desperate streets
Kickstarted our heartbeats
We know hope isn't dead
We can hurt so good again
No matter what we've done
Our black hearts beat as one
Our black hearts beat as one
Our black hearts beat as one
Our black hearts beat as one

ACKNOWLEDGEMENTS

Writing a book might be a solo endeavor, but dragging that puppy kicking and screaming into the world is a different matter altogether. Big thanks to:

Candace Nola and Mort Stone, for their editing prowess.

Lori Michelle, for her incredible formatting.

Marc Vuletich, the artist behind the amazing interior sketches.

Kristina Osborn, for creating a gorgeous cover I fall in love with all over again every time I see it.

Jerry Smith, for scoring the book trailer and coming up with the name "Martyrcycle."

My agent, Jennie Dunham.

Erik Allegoren, Eric Beckrest, and John Porter, for listening to my bullshit over shots of whiskey.

All my writer friends, too many to name, who've been incredible sources of support and inspiration. And to the reviewers and readers as well. I can't tell you how much I appreciate you.

Matt Skiba, Dan Andriano, and Derek Grant, aka The Alkaline Trio, for making the music that helped me get through a bad breakup and teaching me that even famous rock stars get their hearts ripped out. If Modern Love were real, they'd sound a hell of a lot like you guys.

And finally, my Karas and my Evangelines. This book wouldn't exist without you.

ABOUT THIS DUDE

Brian Asman is a writer, actor, director, and producer from San Diego, CA. He's the author of the hit indie novella *Man, Fuck this House* (recently optioned by a major streaming service). His debut novel *Good Dogs* is forthcoming from Blackstone Publishing.

His other books include *I'm Not Even Supposed to Be Here Today* from Eraserhead Press, *Neo Arcana, Nunchuck City, Jailbroke*, and *Return of the Living Elves* from Mutated Media. He's recently published short stories in *Pulp Modern, Kelp,* and *Lost Films*, and comics in *Tales of Horrorgasm.*

A film he co-wrote and produced, *A Haunting in Ravenwood*, is available now on DVD and VOD from Breaking Glass. His short "Reel Trouble" won Best Short Film at Gen Con 2022 and Best Horror Short at the Indie Gathering.

Brian holds an MFA from UCR-Palm Desert. He's represented by Dunham Literary, Inc. Max Booth III is his hype man.

Find him on social media (@thebrianasman) or his website www.brianasmanbooks.com,

Printed in the USA
CPSIA information can be obtained
at www.ICGtesting.com
LVHW011612101023
760307LV00001B/7